THE
BLUE
STOCKING

SUSANNE O'LEARY

Cover design and typesetting by J.D. Smith Design
Edited by Julie McKenzie, Free Range Editorial

CHAPTER 1

The advertisement about the flat seemed to pop up out of nowhere. Not listed in the local paper, it would have gone unnoticed if I hadn't fiddled around on Daft.ie, the national property website. There was a map search I used while looking for a place to live. Not quite sure I was going to stay, I had been living in shared or borrowed accommodation since I'd arrived in Cloughmichael. But as three years had gone by with the speed of light, I felt it was time to put down roots. I liked this town, loved my job, and cherished my new friends. All that was missing was a place I could call home. That day in late May, I took a break from editing and looked up the property site.

There were always a lot of properties for sale but few for rent. That day however, on the usually blank for rent page, I discovered a little blue house icon on the outskirts of town, just where the main road meets the junction to the motorway.

I blinked and squinted at the map. Was it an illusion? I clicked on the icon and got a picture of the property—a 1930s, two-storey house in a street that had escaped my notice on my walks around town.

Spacious two room apartment for rent on ground floor of 1930s villa. Fully fitted kitchen and newly refurbished bathroom. Use of shared garden included in the rent. Long lease. Apply to agency for further details.

I groped for my phone, my eyes still on the ad. This seemed too good to be true. But maybe the flat had been let already?

"Hi," I said when a woman answered. "My name's Audrey Killian, and—"

"—you're calling about the flat for rent?"

"How did you know?"

"Someone told me you were looking for a place."

"What? Who…?" I stopped. No use asking. Everyone knew everyone else's business in this small country town. And they were especially curious about someone like me—a woman running the local newspaper all on her own.

"I wouldn't hang around," the woman said. "It'll be snapped up in no time."

"I'm sure it will be," I agreed. "When can I go and see it?"

"Right away, if you're free."

"Not really. How about tomorrow morning?"

"Too late. Someone is already scheduled to view it then. It's a nice place, so I'm sure it'll be gone after that." She lowered her voice to a bare whisper. "I shouldn't say this, but I'd pop around now if I were you. You might get lucky. The tenant next door has the last say in who gets to rent it, and if she likes you, she might put in a word for you. I'll give her a call and tell her to let you in."

I shot up from my desk. "I'm on my way. Thanks a million for the tip."

"You're welcome. But please don't tell anyone I told you."

"Told me what?" I asked as I walked across the open plan office, where the rest of the staff was busy putting together the Saturday edition of the paper. The woman laughed and hung up.

"Have to go and see a flat before it's gone," I whispered to Dan, our chubby ace photographer and reporter. "Do the layout the way we planned, willya, please? I'll be back before we send it off to the printers."

He nodded, his eyes on the screen. "Grand. That place is great. Needs a lick of paint but…"

I rolled my eyes. "Jesus, is everyone psychic around here?"

Dan shrugged. "Nah, it's just the grapevine or whatever. Chinese whispers and the like. You need a place of your own. Miranda's guest room must feel a little cramped by now."

I sighed. "That's the understatement of the century. Jerry and Miranda must be praying for me to leave by now. I've outstayed my welcome by about a year."

Dan took a bite of the buttered scone beside his mug of tea. "Go on, grab that flat while you can. I'll look after things here."

"You're a star." I squeezed his shoulder. Good old dependable Dan. Always there for me, even if I did rib him about his weight. But he needed it. It was a constant joke between us. "Is that a fat-free scone?" I quipped. "Part of the low-carb diet you started on Monday?"

"Feck off," he replied. "I'll get back on it next weekend."

"Of course you will. But remember what I said: Little pickers wear big knickers."

"Yeah, right," he muttered and turned back to his screen.

"Got to run. But I'll be back for a final check-through." I waved to Mary on the switchboard. "Back in a minute."

I ran down the stairs, narrowly avoiding twisting my ankle, and raced down the street toward the junction and the side road where the woman at the agency had said I'd find the house.

As I slowed down and rounded the corner, I was suddenly aware of the heat on my back. I looked up and saw that the late afternoon clouds had floated away, and the sun was now beating down from a pristine blue sky. After a chilly start, summer was finally here. I took off my denim jacket and draped it over my arm. Tee shirt weather. Shorts and sandals weather. The thought that this flat had a garden made my heart beat faster. My own garden. Barbecues, sun loungers, apple trees, maybe even a little patio for breakfasts and dinners on balmy evenings.

Deep in thought, I turned into a leafy street lined with a row of bungalows and came to a stop at the front gate of a large two-storey house. I looked at the ivy-covered façade, the rose bush at the little gate, the crumbling wall of the front garden and fell in love. The house was like something from a book I'd read as a child. I knew before even reaching the front door I had to live there. It was meant to be.

I pushed at the red door with its brass knocker, feeling that I was entering a whole new phase in my life.

* * *

Inside the dim hall, I found two heavy oak doors facing each other. The one on the left had a small brass plaque that said "Liz Mulcahy." I rang the bell.

After a short wait, the door was opened by a woman dressed in light-blue linen trousers and a white shirt. She had short white hair in little spikes all over her head, and her eyes studied me through delicate gold-framed glasses. She had to be at least sixty, maybe more, but she had that timeless, youthful look of a woman with strict self-discipline. Yoga, swimming, walking flitted through my mind as we looked at each other. I was about to introduce myself, but she beat me to it.

"Audrey Killian? Hello. I'm Liz. You didn't waste any time getting here."

"Hi, Liz." I shook her hand. "I only have a minute. I'm in the middle of—"

"—the Saturday paper? Must be a busy day." She picked up a set of keys from a table by the door. "Let's have a look at your flat, then."

I nodded, my heart beating faster. "Not quite mine yet, of course."

Liz didn't reply but marched across the hall, unlocked the door, and flung it open. "Here we are." She stepped aside. "I think I'll let you discover it on your own. Much better than having someone putting the arm on you to rent it if you don't like it."

I nodded, only half listening, and stepped inside. I jumped as the door banged shut behind me. "You know where to find me when you've had a look around," Liz called through the door. "I'll put the kettle on."

Eager to see every nook and cranny of the flat, I didn't reply. I heard Liz say something else, but her voice became a distant murmur as I walked through the small entrance hall into a large room flooded with sunlight coming through French doors that overlooked a walled garden. The fireplace looked as if it worked, but I'd have to get someone to sweep it before I attempted a fire. Except for two floor-to-ceiling bookcases, the room was unfurnished.

I walked across the wide oak planks to the door and peered out. The garden faced south, and I could see the tips of the Knockmealdown Mountains above the old stones of the wall. This would be the perfect space for Cat. The walls would be too high for her to climb over, and the garden was big enough to provide ample strolling around, climbing on trees, and sniffing at flowers. The lawn needed to be mowed, and the flower beds sported a few straggly daisies among the weeds. There was a greenhouse at the back with a few flower-pots and a long row of things that looked like cucumbers. I glanced at a broken deckchair and a slatted table under the sycamore before I continued my tour.

The kitchen was old-fashioned, but I loved the solid oak cupboards, the marble worktops, and the pale green floor tiles. There was a modern cooker and a fridge with a small freezer compartment. A half-open door led to a larder with a tiny window. Perfect for storing fruit and vegetables and all kinds of food that didn't go in the fridge or freezer. There was no kitchen table, but I had already earmarked my mother's round dining table Dad had said I could have once I had a home of my own. In fact, there was plenty of furniture in his house he'd be glad to part with. He was always telling me he wanted to downsize.

I mentally furnished the living room with the pale blue velvet sofa, the huge armchair, and the little embroidered footstool from my grandmother's house. The bookcases in the living room were perfect for all my books, which I could finally move from my childhood home. "A house is not a home without books," my granny always said.

I breathed in the faint aroma of apples and lamb stew that still lingered in the old kitchen, and continued through a short passage to the bedroom, which, like the living room, faced the garden through the same kind of French windows. I immediately made plans to furnish it with a large bed, a bedside table, and a wardrobe from IKEA. Basic, but cheap. I could jazz it up with bedspreads, throws, and cushions. The bathroom was pretty ordinary but had the requisite bathtub, wash-hand basin, and toilet. Tiled floor in good nick, I noted and also a heated towel rail, handy for drying towels and underwear.

I lingered for a moment on the window seat in the bedroom, the warm sun on my face, and allowed myself to daydream of living in this flat. A mixture of hope and fear filled my mind. What if I couldn't afford the rent? What if someone else proved more suitable? What if Liz didn't feel I was the right person to rent it? What if— "Oh, shut up," I said to myself and went to talk to Liz. She looked like the kind of woman who took no prisoners and would see through any attempt at presenting a false image. Better to tell the truth, the whole truth, and nothing but the truth.

CHAPTER 2

"I love it," I said when Liz opened her door. "I want to live here. I really, really do."

Her silent stare made me babble.

"Okay, so I might not be suitable. I might not even be able to pay the rent. I have a cat, I listen to music, and drink wine. I have no boyfriend right now, but you never know, I might find myself one. I don't smoke, but I cook with spices and garlic, and I love to have friends around." I drew breath.

Liz blinked. Then she burst out laughing. "Oh my God, you really want it, don't you?"

"With every fibre of my being," I said with feeling. "I've never had a place of my own. I'm staying with a friend right now. It was supposed to be a temporary arrangement, but it's lasted more than a year. I'm sure they'll be happy to have their guest room back. And their privacy," I added, thinking of Jerry's increasingly irritated looks in my direction.

Liz moved aside. "Come in. Tea in the garden. I'll tell you all about the house and the owner. And the lease and conditions."

I hesitated. "Oh, but… I have to get back. The paper, the layout…"

"Can they do it without you?"

"Yes, but I'm a control freak. It would give me palpitations to leave them on their own. I might even have a panic attack."

"Maybe you should give it a shot? Leaving them all alone, I mean. What can they do? Put all the photos in upside down?"

I had to laugh. I liked this woman. I knew I had to stay and get all the details about the flat. But the thought of leaving the responsibility of the Saturday paper to Dan, even if he'd seen it done a million times, made me shiver. I hovered on the doorstep for a moment. Then I swallowed and walked inside.

"You're probably right. I should learn to delegate. Excuse me for a moment while I make a phone call." After a quick word with a bewildered Dan, I hung up. "He was a little shell-shocked," I told Liz as I joined her in the kitchen.

She smirked. "I bet he was."

I looked around the kitchen, liking what I saw. Liz had furnished it beautifully with a round pine table, matching chairs, and a marble-topped island in the middle. The windowsill was crammed with herbs in terracotta pots, copper utensils hung from hooks in the ceiling, and a series of coloured glass goblets was displayed on a shelf over the Belfast sink. "What a great kitchen," I exclaimed. "It reflects the 1930s perfectly, even if it's very modern."

"I'm glad you like it." Liz handed me a mug of tea. "Let's sit in the garden under the willow tree, where it's cooler."

Liz's garden was divided from what I was beginning to think of as mine by the short end of the stone wall I had been looking at earlier. This garden, however, was carefully tended, the grass a velvet carpet, the herbaceous borders full of various plants and small bushes in full bloom. I spotted two chairs and a table in the shade of a weeping willow, beside which a stream gurgled over rocks and boulders.

I sat down in one of the chairs and leaned my back against a striped cushion. "What a lovely spot. And you have a stream."

Liz sat down in the other chair. "Yes. That's the one bonus

of this particular flat. The stream disappears into the woods in a bend over there under the little arch in the wall."

"How gorgeous. And how clever the architect was who divided the house into flats. You wouldn't think it was ever a house for just one family."

"It never was. This house was built for apartments. Very unusual at the time, 1937. Just when this country was being established as a sovereign state. But the man who built it had great vision. He wanted to build homes for people who might not be able to afford to buy. There are similar houses in Kilkenny and other smaller towns all over the south. All apartment buildings on a small scale like this, and all rented on a long lease."

I put my mug on the table. "Really? Who was he?"

"Anthony O'Regan. The architect. Quite a legend."

"Of course. I know who you mean. He designed some of the official buildings in Dublin. A bit of a Le Corbusier, wasn't he? Never knew he did this kind of thing, though."

Liz pointed at the upper floor. "His great-grandson lives here. Jonathan O'Regan. Owns this building and a few of the others. He's also an archaeologist. You might have seen him on TV, if you're interested in history."

"Yes, I know who you mean. I loved his series about old houses. In fact, he's one of my favourite TV presenters." My gaze drifted to the upstairs windows, glinting in the sun. There were four of them facing the garden and the hills beyond. "But he has no garden."

"There's a large balcony to the side with nice views of the town. But it doesn't overlook our gardens. This way we're quite private." Liz sat up and directed her gaze at me. "But enough small talk. You want to rent the flat?"

"If I can afford it."

"The rent is four hundred a month, which includes heating and water. Three months payable in advance, plus a security deposit."

"Oh." I thought for a moment. The rent was only just affordable, and the advance and security would have to be taken out of my savings. "That's a bit steep, but worth it. So yes, that's fine. Are there any rules or regulations?"

"No smoking."

"What about my cat?"

"Does she smoke?"

"Not as far as I know."

Liz laughed. "Then she's very welcome. What's her name?"

"Cat."

"Good name. What's she like?"

I smiled. "Black, sleek, and beautiful, and she knows it."

Liz winked. "Just like you?"

I was going to say thank you, then realised it wasn't a compliment but an observation. "Not really," I mumbled.

"I'd say she is. Except you're blonde, of course," Liz added. "But that would be the only difference."

She was right. But she probably didn't know that although I was aware of my looks, I was also aware of their ability to intimidate people, especially men. It was my armour, my weapon. Our eyes met, and I suddenly knew we'd be friends. She had that quiet humour and understanding of older women who had lived and laughed and even cried a little. I wondered if she was married—or ever had been.

"I'm divorced," she said, eerily reading my mind. "My husband left me for someone younger with bigger breasts."

"Oh," was all I managed.

She nodded. "Yes. Happens a lot." She shrugged. "Men. I feel sorry for them sometimes. Don't you?"

"Mm, yes."

"We had no children. I suppose that was part of the problem. He didn't want children. He's in pharmaceuticals. I'm an accountant and worked with him when he started his company. We built it up together. It was our baby, in a way.

All his now. But I started my own little accountancy firm after the divorce, which was a godsend. You have to keep busy when you go through something very painful. I work from home but call around to my clients regularly. That way I get to meet a lot of people. I'm a people person, if you know what I mean."

"Oh, yes. I'm the same. I love people," I said with the feeling we'd be more than just neighbours. Liz seemed like someone who made you want to open up and share your life story. A good listener.

My gaze drifted to a spot by the stream where all kinds of little finches fluttered around a bird table. That high wall between our gardens would prevent Cat from making those little creatures a tasty snack. She had an irritating habit of preying on small birds, bringing them in to me as gifts. A collar with a bell on it might put a stop to that.

As Liz also seemed lost in thought, I got up. "I'd better get back. Do I take it I've been accepted?"

Liz came back to the present. "Yes, of course. Sorry, I should have said. If you call around to the agency, they'll give you the contract to sign. You can move in whenever it suits you. As it's the last day of May next Saturday, how about the following Monday?"

"Perfect. The money for the deposit should have been transferred by then. I'll do it on my phone as soon as I have signed the contract."

"Good. I'll contact Jonathan and let him know he has a new tenant. He's away on a dig in the Midlands right now, excavating the remnants of an Iron Age village. But he gave me his permission to organise the lease and everything with the new tenant." Liz got up and held out her hand. "Let's shake on it then. Welcome to Ivy Gardens."

I smiled as we shook hands. "Thank you. Can't wait to move in."

I said goodbye to Liz and left to walk the short distance

to the agency, where the woman in charge of rentals had the contracts ready, along with a printout of the bank details. It didn't take me long to sign. I transferred the money on my phone, my hands trembling slightly. Parting with that amount in one go was a little scary. But the thought of being in my own home in a little over a week made me forget my fears. It was all worth it. Independence at last. I couldn't wait to tell Dad.

I skipped out of there toward the newspaper office, my heart singing, and my head full of plans for my new abode. Everything around me seemed to have taken on a new gloss. The sun shone, the birds sang, and the slurry-laden breeze smelled like perfume. Nothing could dampen my spirits. Even the faint sound of a siren in the distance didn't penetrate the pink cloud of happiness, until it became so loud I stopped dead. A siren—no, several. What was going on? Something stirred in my journalist brain. A disaster of some kind—a robbery or a car crash? Or even a huge fire? I'd better get to the scene and start reporting.

My phone rang. Still trying to make out where the sounds of the sirens were coming from, I answered it. It was a breathless Dan. I could barely hear him through the din.

"Audrey, come quick," he panted. "We're…we're on fire!"

CHAPTER 3

I ran as fast as my high heels allowed, trying not to believe the worst. Dan had a habit of panicking. He might just mean the kettle had exploded or something. But when I arrived at the building, I realised it was a lot worse than a kettle. Shocked, I stared at the scene.

The whole upper floor of the old Georgian house was aflame. Two fire engines had just arrived, and a third was coming down the street at breakneck speed, all lights blazing, sirens blaring. A huge crowd had gathered, and two Guards were erecting barriers to keep people away from the fire. A small group huddled behind an ambulance, where two paramedics were administering first aid to my staff. At first glance, nobody seemed to have suffered burns or any other physical damage, just mild cases of shock. I homed in on Dan, who was standing as near the blaze as he could, taking photos. An acrid odour hung in the air, and dark clouds of smoke drifted across the street and the surrounding area.

"Holy Mother, what happened?" I shouted over the din.

He turned a soot-stained face to me. "I'm not sure. It spread so fast. One minute, Mary was asking where the stink of burning was coming from, and the next, the whole place was on fire. I think it started in your office. Something was left on—your laptop?"

"What? No, I turned it off before I left. I think," I added.

"Jesus, I knew this would happen one day. I have been *begging* the publisher to let us do the rewiring. They said they'd have to come and inspect it first before they spent the money. This place hasn't been rewired since the 1930s or something—if that."

I scanned the building, trying to assess the damage. It was huge. The whole top floor was gutted. Even if the fire didn't reach the lower floor, the whole building was a total loss.

Glancing at the staff, I saw Mary and Fidelma drinking tea and sobbing quietly. Sinead was trying to comfort them. Mary looked at me with eyes full of sorrow and fear. "The paper," she said. "It's gone. Jerry will be devastated."

I went and put my arm around her. "It'll be all right," I said, trying to sound confident. "We'll find new premises. The insurance will cover everything. Jerry has nothing to do with this. It's the publisher in England who's in charge now."

"I know," she sobbed. "But it was his paper. His family started it all those years ago. This will devastate him."

"I'm sure it will. Did you send the layout to the printers?"

"Yes," she whispered. "It all went off as planned. The Saturday edition will be out as usual tomorrow." She let out a bitter laugh. "As if nothing had happened. All the newspapers will be full of this, except ours. Isn't that ironic?"

We were interrupted by Chief Fire Officer Patrick O'Dea. He was covered in sweat and soot, so different from his usual polished appearance at fundraisers and village fetes. He took off his helmet and wiped his face with his handkerchief. "This is the worst fire in over a decade. But I think we'll be able to put it out. We've called for assistance from Cashel and Clonmel."

I looked up at the flames eating the roof. "There'll be nothing left of it."

"The ground floor will be saved, so anyone can go in and salvage what they can. Lucky there was nobody in any of the shops at the time."

"Nothing to salvage. They were empty because most of those shops have gone out of business," Mary volunteered. "Except for those that moved to the new shopping centre outside Clonmel. *The Knockmealdown News* was the only occupant."

I nodded. "Yes. The new publishing firm were talking about taking over the whole building so we could have our own printers. But that was a long shot. They felt the renovations would cost too much. That and the bloody rewiring," I added under my breath.

O'Dea shot me a look under his bushy eyebrows. "Yes, the old wiring… I have a feeling it will be the main culprit when we take a look in a few days. But as we passed it two years ago, maybe it wasn't that bad?"

I thought for a moment. "It was okay in most of the rooms. But not in my office. There were bare wires that Dan helped me fix with duct tape. Not the best solution, but all we could do while we waited for a decision from the publisher. There was a whole heap of repairs we'd asked to have done."

O'Dea put his helmet back on. "Yeah, well, when big money is involved, security is often compromised. I can hear the other fire engines. Better get back to work. Good day, ladies." He saluted and went to join his men, still struggling to put out the blaze.

The next few hours passed in a daze. I watched the firemen pour thousands of gallons of water on the flames until they finally died down, and all that was left was a smouldering ruin. Everyone around was covered in a film of black dust, and the air was thick with foul smoke. It was like a scene from wartime London.

I managed to climb down from the ambulance, where I had been sitting on a stretcher, as nobody was injured enough to need it. As if in a dream, Jerry appeared beside me, asking the girls if anyone was hurt.

He took my arm. "Jesus, Audrey, what the hell happened?

I just arrived back from Dublin and saw the smoke."

I nodded at the building. "As you can see, we've finally burst into flames. The publisher you sold the paper to thought the rewiring was an unnecessary expense. So here we are. Everything gone."

Jerry looked at the building, his eyes glistening. "A hundred and fifty years," he mumbled as if to himself. "My great-great-grandfather started the paper in that building. We've been through so much since then. Selling the paper was the hardest thing I've ever done. But I thought that way I'd save it. I see I was wrong." He turned to me. "Everything's gone? The archives, all the letters, the photos…?"

I shrugged and leaned against him. "I don't know. I'll have to ask."

"We managed to save your laptop, Audrey," Dan cut in, beside us. "And all the photos are safe. I brought the folders home a couple of days ago. I was going to go through them for the anniversary feature we were planning. The archives are all backed up in the cloud, along with anything really important. We can start up again if we find new premises."

"Someone has to break the bad news to the publisher," I said. "But that's good news, Dan, among all the misery. Well done."

"Not all great news, actually. Saturday's paper is being printed as we speak. There'll be nothing in it about the fire."

"Can we make them stop the presses?" Jerry asked, wiping his eyes with a hanky.

Dan shook his head. "I've tried, but they said no. Not unless we want to rip the whole paper apart."

"I know," I muttered. "Mary just told me. Every paper in the country will have this on the front page, but we'll have—"

"—the final of the schools soccer tournament," Dan said in a near sob. "Ten-year-olds posing for the camera with their proud mammies after the match. I took the photos myself."

"Christ, what a mess," I moaned.

"Even RTE were here," Dan announced. "They filmed the fire and interviewed Mary and Fidelma. They left before you arrived so they could get it in time for the early evening news. You'll be able to watch it on TV in half an hour."

"Fabulous," I muttered.

"Have you called the Montgomery Group in London?"

"I was about to do that," I said. "It's not going to be a very jolly conversation."

"Do you want me to—" Jerry started.

"No. It's my job. I'm the editor-in-chief. This kind of shite comes with the territory." I sighed and hauled my phone out of my pocket. Better to get it over with.

* * *

Christopher Montgomery didn't seem thrilled to be interrupted in the middle of Friday night drinks at the Ritz— or whatever posh watering hole he was at—judging by the laughter and clinking of glasses in the background. I could nearly smell the expensive perfume of the women around him.

"Yes?" he snapped.

"Hi, Christopher. Audrey Killian here," I breezed on, trying to keep the sob out of my voice. "I'm afraid I have some bad news…"

"What? You're not— Hang on a minute." He paused, and I heard him excuse himself to the group. "Yes, go on," he said after a moment's delay. "Bad news? Have you seen a doctor?"

"What?" I asked, confused. "A doctor? What are you talking about? This is Audrey Killian," I repeated. "Editor-in-chief of *The Knockmealdown News* in Cloughmichael. Tipperary, Ireland," I added.

There was a long pause. Then I heard him exhale slowly.

"Ohh. *That* Audrey. Okay. Sorry. I mixed you up with someone else. Similar name, you see."

"I thought that might be the case." In all my misery, I couldn't help letting out a giggle. He was worried some other Audrey was pregnant. I sincerely hoped she wasn't. What a horrible dad he'd make. Then I pulled myself up and prepared to tell him my own very bad news. "I'm sorry, Christopher, but I'm afraid there's been a fire in the office here."

"How bad is it?"

"Very bad."

"Give me the whole story."

"The building is destroyed. We have no office as such right now."

I could hear him breathe on the other end. "Fuck," he snapped. "That's truly awful. That paper was performing better than any of our local newspapers in the whole of the British Isles."

I bristled. "We're not British, we're Irish."

"Yes, okay. I'd be grateful if you didn't trot out your patriotism right now. Can you find new premises?"

"I don't know. I'm standing here looking at the blackened remains of our office in a listed Georgian building. We're all very upset, as you can imagine. Nobody was hurt, by the way. But I suppose that would be a minor detail to you." I stopped. Shit, what was I doing? Insulting the publisher? He could fire me on the spot. "Sorry, didn't mean to—"

"Never mind," Christopher snapped in a way that told me he was anxious to get back to the Friday night revelling. "I'll have to come out there, won't I?" As if he were being forced to go to the Outer Hebrides in the middle of winter.

A cold hand squeezed my heart. "No, that's not really nece—"

"I'll be there Monday," he interrupted. "I'll expect you to have found alternative premises for the paper by then. Meet me at Killybeg House hotel at five pm." He hung up without saying goodbye.

I put away my phone, my heart sinking. I wasn't looking forward to that meeting. And if I didn't come up with a solution for at least a temporary office, he'd probably fire me. I looked from Jerry's slumped form and ashen face to Mary and Fidelma sobbing in each other's arms. My gaze met Dan's worried eyes. "Don't worry, gang. It'll be all right," I promised, trying to sound cheerful. "We'll find a new office and keep going."

"How?" Dan asked.

I patted his shoulder. "If there's a will, there's a way, you know. And there certainly is a will, isn't there?"

"Yes," Mary said, wiping her tears. "Of course there is!"

I grinned. "That's the spirit! *The Knockmealdown News* will rise again," I declared, my fist in the air, trying to believe my feisty words. It wasn't going to be easy. Added to all the misery, I had just spent nearly all my savings on three months' rent for a flat I might not be able to live in. The prospect of meeting Christopher Montgomery didn't fill me with joy either. How the hell was I going to come up with new premises by Monday?

CHAPTER 4

Later that night, when I had retired to my room with my only slightly damaged laptop, Cat purring on my bed, the phone rang.

Please, not Christopher Montgomery, I thought, glancing at the caller ID. But it was my dad.

"Audrey?" he said in that way that always makes me feel guilty I haven't replied to his e-mails. "Are you all right? I've just seen the evening news and the fire."

I turned off my laptop and got up from the desk. "I'm fine, Dad. I wasn't even in the office when the fire broke out."

"Where were you? I thought Friday was the busiest day of the week for you."

"It is." I walked across the room and curled up on the bed. This was going to be a long conversation. "But I was taking a break to look at a flat for rent."

"Oh, good. You need a place of your own. Did you take it?"

"Yes, yes. And I paid three months' rent in advance. But the fire and the office... It's awful. Luckily, nobody was hurt, but the building was destroyed. Poor Jerry's in bits. The paper has been run from that house since his great-great-grandfather started it. And I had to tell that bastard of a publisher what happened, and he's coming here on Monday, expecting me to have found somewhere for us to work now that we have no office, and—" I suddenly burst into tears. "I don't know what to do," I wept.

There was a brief silence. Then I heard Dad take a deep breath. "You're going to pull yourself together, Audrey," he said in that stern voice he used to address people who had run up a big overdraft. "You're going to blow your nose and stop snivelling. Then you're going to go out and find some kind of office, even if it's in a barn. Do you hear me?"

"Yes, Dad," I whispered.

"Good. And if you decide to cancel the flat, come and live with me. It's only an hour and a half from there, after all. Lots of people have a longer commute than that."

"God, no," I said. The thought of moving back to live with my dad made me feel sick. I'd get a lecture every day about my lack of ambition and how women my age out there were running companies and having brilliant political careers. Managing a country newspaper didn't quite count as having made it to the top. "Thanks. I'll be fine. I'll either stay here or—" I jumped up from the bed. "It's okay, Dad. I'll be fine."

"Are you sure?" he asked, his voice more gentle. "I'd love to have you. It'd be like old times, when you were a teenager and we used to read by the fire."

"I'm nearly thirty-three years old, Dad, not fourteen."

"I know," he grunted, as if regretting his slightly emotional suggestion earlier. "Time flies by so fast. I'll be a granddad before you know it."

I had to laugh. "Not in the foreseeable future, I'm afraid. I have to meet Mr Right first."

"That seems to be very low on your list of priorities. Any sign of a possible candidate?"

"Not at the moment. But I'll send out a newsflash when there is."

"Don't hang around," he warned. "The biological clock…"

I rolled my eyes. "Please, stop. Don't be a mother hen. It doesn't suit you."

He changed tacks. "You didn't reply to my e-mail."

"You mean the one where you listed the six top earners among women in Ireland? All my age and all earning more than half a million a year?"

"Yes. I thought it might inspire you to get your ass back to Dublin and get yourself a proper job. You have the qualifications, Audrey. I should know. I paid for them."

"I do have a proper job. I'm happy here. Does that not count? Don't you want me to be happy?"

"Happiness is overrated. Your mother used to say—"

"Mum's dead," I said flatly. "She's been dead a long time." My mother had gone for a walk one cold winter afternoon and never come back. She had been killed by a hit-and-run driver. I was seven. I still remember sitting at the bottom of the stairs in our house in Abbeyleix waiting for her. I sat there for hours, not understanding the commotion, the tears, the shouting. Then Dad had to tell me. I shivered despite the warm evening.

"I know," he whispered. "I'm sorry."

"So how's the bank going?" I breezed on. "Lots of new customers?"

"It's quite busy. Two new companies are opening their offices here. More jobs, more people moving into town. We're only an hour from Dublin, so it's getting popular to live here."

"And what about your personal life? Are you getting me a lovely stepmother soon?"

"Not very likely. I was seeing this woman, but…"

I knew what had happened. My mother—or her memory—got in the way. It always did. Poor old Dad had never got over the loss of his beautiful young wife. I don't think he ever would. "Don't worry," I soothed. "It'll happen when it's meant to. I believe in fate."

"Sometimes fate seems busy elsewhere. Anyway, glad you're all right. Good night, Audrey."

"'Night, Dad."

I shook my head and hung up. Poor Dad, all alone with his memories. Just like me: a lone wolf, unable to find that special someone. He was too sad, I was too picky. Not that I didn't hope I'd meet someone to live happily ever after with, but it wasn't likely to happen anytime soon. Unless fate, or Karma, kicked in with a vengeance.

* * *

The phone rang again as I was getting ready for bed. I picked up without checking the caller ID. "Dad, what now?"

"Audrey?" said a voice I didn't quite recognise. "This is Liz Mulcahy. We met at the flat earlier. Just wanted to know if you're all right. That was a terrible fire."

"I'm fine, but the office is gone, I'm afraid. Huge problem for us. We have to find something temporary so we can keep working."

"I see." She paused. "You know what? I think I have an idea… Not my place to suggest it, but… Can you come here tomorrow morning? Jonathan has just arrived for the weekend, and he wants to meet you. Then I can tell you what just occurred to me."

"Jonathan?"

"Jonathan O'Regan. The owner. Your landlord."

"Oh, of course. Sorry. So much has happened that I kind of forgot about him being my landlord. I'll be there at nine if that would suit you."

"Perfect. See you then." She hung up before I had a chance to ask what her idea was.

I went to bed feeling that there might be a ray of hope and that maybe Karma was beginning to happen. At least in some small way.

* * *

Jonathan O'Regan was delightful. That was the first thought that shot into my mind as I shook his hand. He was even better looking in real life than on TV. His regular features, kind eyes, and warm smile were devoid of any calculation or flirtation. He was just a very nice man. Around my age— maybe a little older—he was slim and tall with short, light-brown hair. His hazel eyes had a slightly distant look, as if he were thinking about a book he had just read or planning to write some learned document about life in mediaeval Ireland. He was nattily dressed in white linen trousers, a blue fitted shirt, and tennis shoes, which made him look like something from *The Great Gatsby*. I had seen him on TV presenting historical programmes and loved his voice and unassuming manners.

"Hello, Audrey. Nice to meet you," he said as he took my hand, sounding as if he meant it.

"And you, Jonathan," I replied and returned his friendly smile. "I've watched all your programmes on TV. I love history, so every one was a treat."

He blushed slightly. "Thank you. That's good to hear. I'm so sorry about the fire," he continued. "What a horrible thing to happen. I hope nobody was hurt?"

I sighed. "No, thank God."

"At least that's something to be happy about." He turned to Liz, hovering in her doorway in the hall. "How about a cup of coffee in my flat? We could sit on the terrace as it's such a beautiful morning."

She nodded. "Good idea. If we had croissants, we could pretend we were in France."

Jonathan smiled. "You know what? I have some in the freezer. Won't take me long to warm them in the oven. Please, follow me." He turned and started running up the stairs in easy strides.

Liz laughed and slammed her door shut. "Come on, Audrey. You'll love his flat. And wait till you see the terrace, it's been done up for the summer. It's wonderful."

"Nice guy," I said.

"He's charming. Very close to his feminine side, if you see what I mean."

"Oh. Okay." So Jonathan was gay? Not that it mattered in the slightest, it might even be an advantage if we were to become friends. No sexual tension or any kind of expectations from either of us.

As I followed Liz up the stairs, I was struck by how much younger she looked this morning. She wore a loose-fitting navy linen shift and espadrilles with ribbons wound around her slim ankles, her hair in little curls around her face. She must have been beautiful when she was young. *No, beautiful now*, I corrected myself. Why assess people the way they used to be?

We arrived at Jonathan's apartment and found the door wide open, classical music wafting through a bright living room filled with books and stacks of CDs. The furniture was a charming mishmash of old and new, the worn oriental carpet littered with pieces of paper.

"Please step over the mess," Jonathan called from the open door of the terrace. "I'm putting together my notes from the dig. The best way to get an overview for editing is to put all the bits of writing on the floor."

"I know," I said, carefully stepping around the sheets of paper. "I do the same when I have something long to edit. I even cut out sections and organise them like a jigsaw puzzle. I think it's called 'reverse outline' or something." I stopped at the terrace door. "What an incredible place," I exclaimed, gobsmacked by the sights and smells.

I had never seen such a gorgeous outdoor space. There were palm trees and exotic plants in pots around a seating arrangement with cushions in vivid colours. The terracotta tiles and the sundial gave the terrace a Mediterranean air, and the jasmine bush emitted a heavenly scent. A striped awning protected us from the hot sun, and the warm breeze brought with it the smell of fresh bread and coffee. Awe-struck, I sank down among the cushions of one of the chairs.

Liz laughed. "What did I tell you?"

"Did you do all this?" I asked Jonathan as he arrived with a tray.

"Most of it, yes. I got someone from the garden centre to do the tiling."

"I love the sundial."

"I nicked that from Liz's garden. Sorry, Liz."

Liz poured herself coffee. "That was before I moved in. I have no right to complain, even if it would have been nice to have it. But it's so perfect here, and Jonathan is kind enough to let me sit here on hot evenings. Coolest place in the house, as it faces east."

I took a warm croissant from the plate Jonathan offered me. "But Irish summers are so unpredictable. I can't imagine that this stuff would survive a day with high winds and rain."

"Most of it can be moved indoors," Jonathan remarked. "I keep a close eye on the weather."

"We're supposed to have a long hot summer this year." Liz bit into her croissant.

I nodded. "So I heard. Not that I believe it, but let's hope it's true."

Jonathan sat down in the deckchair opposite me. "But we have things to discuss. When do you think you'll be moving in?"

I struggled to sit up. "I was thinking Monday, but now with the fire and everything, I'm not sure I can. I have to find some other place for the staff to work, and that's not going to be easy."

"That's where I come in," Liz interrupted. "I should have asked you before, Jonathan, but I was thinking that the flat next door to this one might suit as temporary accommodation for the paper."

Jonathan stared at her. "What? The— But that's my cousin's apartment."

"Yes, but he's not actually living there, is he?" Liz argued. "The flat's been empty since he moved to New York six months ago. Maybe he'd agree to let it until he comes back?" She turned to me. "How big an office do you need?"

I thought for a moment. The flat in question must be similar to mine in size and layout. It would work, if we made the living room into a communal space. I could take the bedroom as my office. "It would be fine, actually," I said. "Just about. The only problem would be phone lines. We need at least three."

"Could you operate with just one and a few extensions?" Liz asked. "And of course you all have mobiles."

I nodded. "Yes. That would be okay."

Jonathan looked from Liz to me. "Seems like it's all decided. But yes, I think we could at least see if my cousin agrees. The flat has very little furniture, but all you need are a few desks and chairs, right?"

"Something like that," I mumbled, wondering how much of the office furniture could be salvaged from the wreck. "Oh God, our computers. Dan had just got a new big screen for the layouts and photos. Must be all gone."

"Won't the insurance cover that?" Jonathan asked.

I shrugged. "Probably. I haven't looked into that stuff yet. Jerry owns the building, but the publisher is responsible for the insurance of the contents. They worked it out together. I'm meeting him on Monday," I said glumly. "The publisher, I mean. He wants me to have new premises by then. Or he'll fire me."

"Did he say that?" Jonathan asked.

"Not in so many words."

Jonathan reached across the coffee and croissants and

patted my hand. "It'll be okay. I'll call Tony—my cousin—in a few hours, when it's morning over there. I'm sure he'll agree."

He was right. A few hours later, Tony, who was working for a big company in New York, had agreed to let his apartment to *The Knockmealdown News* for the same rent as I was paying for my apartment. The lease would be renewable every year, and there would be a clause to terminate the contract should Tony want to move back—highly unlikely, I was told.

I inspected the premises with Jonathan and saw that it was indeed perfect for a small operation such as ours. We could move in straight away, as soon as the contract was signed, and I could move into mine the following Tuesday. *Fate*, I thought, as I skipped down the street back to Miranda's guest room, *has finally kicked in*.

But the glow faded very quickly. That evening, on my way home from a meeting over drinks with the staff, I got a call from Pat O'Dea.

"Audrey, I have some news," he started. "Kind of worrying, really."

"Yes, what?"

"Well... I don't want to upset you, but—"

"Stop messing, Pat. Tell me what's up."

He made a sound like a gulp. "We suspect the fire was your fault."

CHAPTER 5

I froze to the spot. "What are you talking about? My fault?"

"Yes, I'm afraid it looks that way now. The plug behind your desk was all burnt out. You must have left something on and forgotten. A laptop, a heater…"

"A heater. In this weather?"

"A fan, then?"

"I don't—didn't even have a fan."

"Well, whatever was plugged into that socket started the fire, that's all we know now."

"Shit."

"Yeah. It wouldn't have happened if the wiring weren't so old."

"Have you told Jerry?"

"No, I thought you—"

"You tell him, Pat. It's your job."

He sighed. "Right. I will, so."

"Thanks."

"But you have to tell your boss. That English publisher guy. That's *your* job."

"Gee, thanks for reminding me." I hung up, realising I'd have to take the flak when I got back to Miranda's. Then there'd be a whole evening of woe. Thank God I was moving out in a couple of days.

I picked up my phone again. I'd better get my things

over to the flat as soon as it could be arranged. I had already placed an order with IKEA for the bedroom furniture. After having agreed with Dad that he'd rent a van and get all the stuff I wanted from home delivered on the following Tuesday evening, I walked into the house ready to face Jerry. He'd be devastated not only by the loss of that building, but also by the fact that it might have been my fault.

But was it really an accident? Or had someone fiddled with something in my office? A prank that had turned nastier than the culprit intended? But who? And why? I opened the door, walked into the house, and heard Jerry shouting. Pat must have just told him the news.

Disbelieving, he stood in the middle of the living room, staring at me. "What the hell happened, Audrey? Did you leave something on when you went out?"

"No. I'm sure I didn't. I always switch off my laptop before going out. I don't want anyone touching it."

"It was the wiring, wasn't it? Why on earth didn't the publisher agree to have it done? It was his responsibility according to the contract we signed. I own the building, but he swore that he'd look after any repairs. Why did this have to happen?"

"I don't know," I whispered and put my arms around him.

After hugging me tight, he stepped away. "*The Knock-mealdown News* will keep going, won't it, Audrey? Don't let it die. Promise me that."

I held up my hand in a scout's salute. "I swear."

* * *

I hadn't seen Killybeg House since its glitzy inauguration at Christmas. It hadn't been quite finished then and only started to receive guests three months later. We had done a big feature, as had many of the national newspapers. Beautifully restored and furnished, it deserved all the accolades. It would be Ireland's most glamorous country hotel, rivalled only by Mount Juliet.

I drove past the gatehouse, where I lived when I was managing the house before the big auction. The owner, Richard Hourigan, and his brand new wife, Pandora, were now staying there. "Just for the summer," Pandora had assured me when we'd met briefly at the gym. "Just while everything is being established."

I realised she was used to better things than our little country town, being a New York socialite and heiress to a considerable fortune. She was only a temporary member of the little gym before the spa and all its high-tech facilities were finished.

A statuesque brunette with green eyes, Pandora wasn't the typical trophy wife. She was chubby and chatty with a great sense of humour. Everyone at the hotel loved her, I'd heard. Her charm and beauty, combined with several millions of a future inheritance, must have made her an irresistible package. The only mystery was why on earth she had fallen for Richard Hourigan.

I drove up to the entrance. A young man in hotel livery immediately ran down the steps and offered to park my car. I got out, tossed him the keys to my battered Toyota, and sauntered into the lobby. There was nobody around except the woman in reception, who turned out, to my surprise, to be Pandora.

"Hi, Audrey," she said and patted my hand. "So sorry about the fire and everything."

"Thanks, Pandora."

"I hope this won't mean the end of our newspaper."

"Not at all," I said with great emphasis. "We'll keep going no matter what. We've even found a new office already."

"That's fantastic!"

"But why are you here, playing receptionist?"

Pandora laughed, tossing her glossy hair behind her shoulders. "We haven't got a permanent one yet. I'm still interviewing applicants. We need someone who speaks several languages and has a bit of experience. In the meantime, I have something to do besides talking to Richard's boring friends who fly in from New York to play golf and have their nails done. And that's only the men. The women..." She rolled her eyes.

I laughed. "I get the picture."

"But I'm loving running the hotel. I never had a real job before, and this is so much fun. And this town and the people are so darling. I thought living in an Irish country town would bore me to death, but it's actually more interesting than the big city. Richard wants to go back to New York once the hotel is running smoothly, but he's going to have a fight on his hands."

"That's nice to hear." I checked my watch. "I'll catch up with you later, Pandora. I have a meeting in a few minutes."

"I know. I believe Mr Montgomery is expecting you in the bar." She winked. "Very sexy, isn't he?"

"In a scary way." I smoothed my skirt. Was it a tad short for a business meeting? But it was a hot day, and I hadn't had time to change. In any case, I needed all my weapons for this particular encounter. I checked that my hair was still in a tight bun and ran a finger under my eyes to remove any mascara smudges. "Wish me luck," I said to Pandora.

"Good luck, Audrey," she whispered before she turned to a guest who had just appeared at the desk.

With his dark curly hair, crooked nose, and thin mouth, Christopher Montgomery was not a handsome man. But he was sexy. *God, yes, sexy as hell*, I thought when I spotted him sitting at a table by the open window, sipping from a champagne flute, a bottle of Bollinger in a cooler beside him. He was dressed in white shorts that showed off his muscular thighs and a golf shirt with the crocodile logo that clung to his slightly sweaty chest. I steeled myself to adopt a professional air and walked toward him. He looked up as I approached, giving my legs a brief, appreciative glance.

"About time," he grunted and got up to shake my hand.

I glanced at my watch. "Two minutes late. I'm dreadfully sorry."

"Yeah, right." He sat down and gestured at the bottle. "How about a cold drink? It's a hot day."

"Thanks. I'll have a bottle of water."

He raised an eyebrow. "Really? You don't like champagne?"

I sat down. "Love it. But not while working."

"Oh." He clicked his fingers at a passing waiter and ordered a bottle of Ballygowan. Then he took another sip of his champagne and turned back to me. "What have you got for me? Good news, I hope."

"Good and bad."

"Give me the good news."

I pulled the contract from my bag and started to speak very fast to cover up the effect he was having on me. "I found new premises for the paper. Just temporary, but a great space with enough room for everyone. It's an apartment not far from the old office. The owner has agreed to a short let until we can find something more permanent. I have the contract here for you to sign, and then we can move in tomorrow. We have already drawn up a layout for the Wednesday edition that will be published as usual, only a little slimmed down, of course." I drew breath and handed him the contract.

Christopher glanced through the three pages and nodded. "Okay. Great stuff. Tomorrow, you said?"

I squirmed as his eyes bored into mine. "Well, we've already taken possession of the space and started working. The owner of the building lives next door, and he said it'd be okay. We only have one phone line and our own personal

35

laptops, so we were hoping you could give me the go-ahead to replace some of the equipment we lost in the fire. And allow me to buy a few desks and chairs."

"Hmm. And the bad news?"

"It's about the fire." I swallowed the lump in my throat. "It appears that it was caused by the old wiring. So, in a way it was your fault."

He stared at me. "What?"

"The rewiring should have been done ages ago. You dragged your heels about that, remember? And now the old wiring appears to have been the cause of the fire."

"Who says?"

"The fire department. There's an investigation and—"

He slammed his glass on the table. "I'll expect a full report tonight. This might affect the insurance. I have to look up the policy and see if there's a clause about such an event. If there is, we might not get compensation. And in that case—" he paused "—I can't give you the go-ahead for any kind of purchase right now."

I crossed and recrossed my legs. "So we're supposed to sit on the floor and use our phones to get that paper out?"

He glanced at my legs again. "Or we could just close it down for a few weeks until the insurance stuff is sorted. Maybe you'd like a little holiday? Do you play golf?"

"Close it down?" I asked incredulously, my professional hat firmly back on. "That would kill us. It would take months to get the circulation back to where it was before the fire. And no, I haven't played golf since I was twelve, when my uncle brought me to a driving range at his club. You can't be serious about closing down the paper. Even if it was for a week, you'd seriously damage circulation numbers."

"I might even close it down altogether," Christopher stated. "It seems like a lame duck right now. Losing money with all these expenses."

I met his dismissive gaze with a cold stare. "You can afford to keep it going, Christopher. Your publishing empire makes millions each year, I read in the *Financial Times* recently. Surely you could stretch to a few thousand to get us the basic equipment to get back to work?"

He laughed and put a hand on my knee. "The *Financial Times*? Aren't we the smart cookie?"

Trying not to let the contact with his warm hand unnerve me, I picked it up with my thumb and index finger and dropped it in his lap. "I'm not a cookie."

"Of course not, you're a very clever girl."

I got up. "No, I'm a woman."

"You're very beautiful, whatever you are."

"Thank you. Listen, Christopher, I've said what I came to say, so—"

"You're leaving?" He leaned back and stroked the neck of the champagne bottle. "Are you sure you wouldn't like to stay for a little…bubbly?"

I closed my eyes for an instant, the picture of us in a huge double bed flitting through my mind. "Positive," I snapped, more annoyed at myself than him. I pointed at the documents on the table. "If you'll sign that contract, I'll leave and get back to work. I have a paper to get out. That is, unless you really want to close it down. But, in my humble opinion, that wouldn't be a wise move. I have plans, big plans to increase our circulation even more."

"Really?"

"Yes." I hauled out a pen from my bag and handed it to him. "Here, sign, and we have a deal."

"For what?" He drawled.

"For me rescuing the paper from the ashes and earning you even more money."

"Okay." He scribbled his signature on the contract and handed it to me. "There. So what is this plan of yours? Would you care to sit down and tell me about it?"

I pushed the contract into my bag. "I'll e-mail it to you. Must go. Have a safe trip back to London."

He waved a lazy hand in my direction. "I'm not going back just yet. I'm going to stay around for a while. This is a great place. The weather is terrific, and I just found myself some fabulous golf partners. Maybe we could get together one evening when you're not so…busy?"

"That would take a while." I took a deep breath. Holy shit, he was not leaving. I hoped he'd stay out of my way. How long would it take before he managed to break down my defences and seduce me?

"I'm sure you could find a little time to have fun."

"See you, Christopher," I said and walked away, fighting with my hormones and my libido.

"Just a minute," he said, his voice dropping the languid tone.

I stopped and turned. "Yes?"

He gazed at me. "I believe I just signed a contract for three months of temporary office space?"

"Eh, yes."

"And you asked for permission to replace some of the equipment that was lost in the fire?"

"That's right." I waited while he seemed to consider what to say next.

After a long silence, he finally nodded as if he were granting me some magic wish. "Okay. Here's *my* deal: You turn that paper around and three months from now have the circulation above what it was before the fire. I'll give you two thousand to get the basics of whatever you need in electronic equipment. But if, when the three months are up, the paper is no longer making a considerable profit—" another long pause while I held my breath "—*The Knockmealdown News* will be closed down."

I stiffened. That was a hell of a tall order. "That's not—" I started but closed my mouth mid-rant. No use arguing.

He lifted that eyebrow again. "You were going to say…?"

"Nothing. Fine. I'll be in touch. Bye." With that, I marched off, my heels clicking against the marble floor, feeling I had been handed a deal nobody should have to accept by a man I found dangerously attractive.

He'd given me three months. I'd have to rescue the paper and increase circulation by the end of the summer or we would all be unemployed. Could I do it? I nodded to myself as I waited for my car to be brought around by the valet. *Yes, I can and I will*, I thought. I just had to come up with that killer plan. And stay away from trouble in the form of a very sexy man.

CHAPTER 6

"I need a plan," I said to Jonathan later that evening.

He had poked his head into the new office while I was making a list of furniture and equipment we needed. He'd invited me for a drink on his gorgeous terrace, which I'd accepted at once. I needed a friend to talk to. I hadn't known him more than a few days, but I had felt a strange affection for him at first glance. I knew immediately he'd be someone I could trust. Gay men make the best friends. There's an extra dimension to them that straight men don't have. Perhaps it's that feminine side, but they know the meaning of true friendship. That's exactly how I felt about Jonathan. And he was nice-looking too.

I relaxed against the cushions in a deckchair on his terrace, sipping wine and looking at the streetlights all over town and the deep pink clouds floating above the tops of the mountains beyond. There was a whiff of barbecued meat in the air, mingling with the scent of honeysuckle brought in by the light breeze. Summer smells.

Jonathan turned on the electric lanterns at the edge of the terrace and lit the candles on the small table between us. "Do you want to stay for something to eat? I was going to toss a few prawns on the grill, and I've more than enough for two. With salad and bread and my homemade garlic mayonnaise. What do you say?"

I laughed. "I'm drooling already. Yes, please." I stretched and sighed. "Thank you for inviting me. I need a little TLC before all the work tomorrow. Moving into two places at once isn't going to be easy."

"When's your dad coming with your furniture?"

"About eleven tomorrow morning. The furniture store in Cashel has promised to deliver the desks and chairs for the office by nine. I'll be able to have a staff meeting and get everyone working on the Wednesday paper before I get stuck into my own flat. Then we'll have to manage with whatever laptops we have until we can replace the PCs and the big screen for the layout."

Jonathan topped up his glass from the bottle of Pinot Grigio. "So, what kind of plan do you need?"

"Something that will increase circulation really fast. We were doing well before the fire, but the publisher has now given me an ultimatum. Make him some mega bucks, or we'll all get the chop."

"Sounds like a real shit."

I drained my glass. "That's for sure. I just had a less than pleasant meeting with him at Killybeg. The problem is—I fancy him. I think the feelings are mutual. I'm a sucker for alpha males. He seemed to guess how I felt too, which is embarrassing to say the least. Shit." I sighed and reached for the bottle.

Jonathan glanced at my legs. "Maybe a more demure outfit might have been better?"

I tugged at my skirt. "I didn't have a chance to change. Been rushing around all day, and then I had a staff meeting at the pub."

Jonathan leaned back in his chair and smiled. "But your amazing looks are probably your best…ahem, asset, right? Your weapons of mass seduction?"

I had to laugh. "Spot on, my friend. God, this will sound so precious, but okay, I use my looks to get ahead in business. Does that sound really tarty to you?"

He smiled. "No. I think women have a tough time out there in career-land. It's hard to compete in a man's world. Why not use whatever you have? I call that power. You have what intimidates men most—a sharp brain inside a beautiful body they can't have. I bet you've been laughing behind the poor suckers' backs while getting the best stories and the best deals."

I chuckled. "Of course I have. In business anyway. In my personal life it doesn't work very well. My love life is less than exciting."

"I find that hard to believe. What the hell is wrong with those guys?"

I let out a bitter laugh. "What's wrong with me, you mean? There must be something missing. Only last year—" I couldn't go on. Remembering what had happened with Marcus made my eyes sting. "Never mind. It's still hard to talk about it."

"I'm sorry."

"Thanks. I'm trying my best to get over it, but it still hurts. Deep down I know it was my fault. I'm too bossy, too opinionated. Men don't like that. Especially those alpha males I have the irritating habit of falling for." I stopped, surprised at myself. I would never have admitted my weakness for domineering bastards to anyone else, but I had this strange feeling about Jonathan. As if we'd met before, or were meant to meet, and that he had been waiting for me all my life so I could share my secrets with him. I shook my head. Crazy thoughts. Must be the wine.

As if reading my mind, he got up. "We need food. We must be getting light-headed from the wine."

I nodded. "Yes. Food would be good. Do you need a hand?"

"No. Just relax. I'll be back in a minute."

While Jonathan put the meal together in the kitchen, I put my hands behind my head and looked up at the stars glinting in the darkening sky. What a haven this was, away from stress and misery. And Jonathan. Like a long-lost brother.

"I was an only child," I said when Jonathan came back with a platter of grilled prawns. "My mother died when I was seven."

"Must have been hard." He put the platter on the table. "Let me just get the salad and bread, and you can tell me about it."

I hesitated when he came back. Why ruin his evening with the story of my life? But as we ate, Jonathan prompted me to talk. "Must have been hard to lose your mother at such an early age. But you had your dad."

"More like he had me," I replied. "He leaned on me for support those first years. I was glad to help. But it made me grow up very fast."

"I can imagine. Not fair really, to steal your childhood like that."

"I never thought of it like that, but it's true in a way," I said, remembering the dolls and toys forgotten in my room while I helped Dad to cook dinner and did other little chores to make his life easier. "I turned to books for comfort. It turned me into a bookworm."

"I know what you mean." Jonathan topped up my glass and divided the last of the prawns between us. "I was one too. I was an only child like you. My parents were both in their forties when I was born. They had no more children. I was shy and a bit of a nerd and had few friends. So I disappeared into the world of books."

"Pity we didn't meet then. I wasn't shy, but I was very prickly. A real teacher's pet too, which didn't make me very popular." I chewed on a piece of bread, remembering. "My dad was very ambitious for me. Pushed me to do my best at all times."

"And you did, I bet."

"Yes. I enjoyed it too. Loved university. More books, you know?"

He laughed. "Yeah. Sounds like you were a cool kid, like me."

"Ha ha, yes. I was this tall, geeky girl with glasses who couldn't stop lecturing people. Not your dream date."

His gaze scanned my body. "Then what happened?"

"I was thrown into the world of journalism. I realised very quickly that good looks will get you the entrée to a lot of well-known people. And that they—especially men—are more inclined to spill the beans to a good-looking woman than a plain one. At that same time, I got a job at *Image* magazine, which gave me a taste for fashion. Started using contact lenses and learned how to dress to impress. Fun times."

"And it gave you the confidence you have now," Jonathan added.

I leaned back against the cushions. "Yes, I suppose. Superficially. It's an armour I can hide behind. Deep down I'm still that nerdy little girl."

We talked late into the night, sharing stories of our childhoods, our parents, summer holidays, interests—and books. Many of Jonathan's favourites were the same as mine—Thomas Hardy, Jane Austen, Thackeray, and the Russian classics. We were deep into an argument about whether Anna Karenina and Madame Bovary were spoilt bitches or simply women stuck in loveless marriages when my eyes started to close. I yawned.

"I'd better go back to Miranda's to get some sleep."

Jonathan pulled himself from the depths of his chair. "I'll walk you there."

"That would be lovely, but you don't have to. You must be tired."

"I'm fine. I've been writing all day. A bit of exercise will do me good before bed."

We walked slowly through the silent streets, with Jonathan's arm resting lightly on my shoulders. It felt comforting to be with a man who just wanted to be friends. Someone who was cuddly and warm and supportive.

I stopped at Miranda's gate. "Here we are. Thanks for taking me home." I gave him a warm hug and sighed. "Oh, it's so nice to do this, just hugging and feeling close. You're like a big warm teddy bear, Jonathan." I looked up at his face, dimly illuminated by the streetlight. "Thank you for taking me home and for the yummy dinner."

He laughed and ruffled my hair. "You're an article, Audrey, as my mother used to say. I've never met a girl like you. But I'm glad I did. Good night. Sweet dreams."

He kissed my cheek and walked away into the darkness, whistling a tune I vaguely recognised. I sighed and floated in through the door, up the stairs, and into bed. A day that started so badly had ended so well. A new home and a new friend—a forever friend.

* * *

Moving day started with the delivery of the office furniture, which, with the help of the rest of the staff, was soon in place. We set up our laptops and got to work on the Wednesday paper. Dan had uploaded the photos he took of the fire to our website with a brief post. There wasn't much else we could do, as the national newspapers and TV and radio news had been full of it all evening the day of the fire.

"Brilliant work, Dan," I said. "I saw what you put up on the Facebook page too. I think we can move on now, if we're all happy that we've covered every angle of this disaster, including our move here."

I decided not to share what Pat O'Dea had told me, as I had no idea what the forensic team had come up with.

I looked at my staff as they sat at their new desks, coping with the lack of equipment as best they could. What a great bunch they were. We had been working together for over three years, ever since Finola appointed me to the position of editor-in-chief with Jerry's approval. Mary, Fidelma, and Sinead, all local girls who knew everyone in town and what people wanted from a country newspaper. And dear old Dan, excellent photographer and layout man. The best team any editor could wish for. How sad it would be if they all lost their jobs. But I was determined to make sure that wouldn't happen. Not on my watch anyway.

I cleared my throat, standing in the middle of what had become the communal office. "Listen, gang, we have to think hard about getting this paper to sell even more copies than before. The darling publisher has told me that we have three months to increase circulation or—" I ran my finger across my throat.

There was a stunned silence. "Shit," Fidelma said. "The gobshite."

I nodded. "I agree. But there you are. He's the boss, we're the minions. Our jobs are on the line." I waved my hands in the air. "Come on, think!"

"I have a kind of idea," Fidelma piped up. "You might think it's stupid but—"

"Spit it out," I urged. "We need to throw everything out there. Good ideas, bad ideas, whatever ideas. Then we'll sort them out and see if there are any nuggets of gold in there."

Fidelma nodded. "Okay, so, don't laugh, but I thought we could do a digital paper. We could have our own app and—"

"Our own app," Mary jeered. "Where are you going to get that, then? That could cost a lot of money."

"My cousin knows how to do it," Fidelma said. "He developed his own app for a game he invented. He might do one for us."

I looked at Fidelma. "Okay. So where are we going with this?"

Fidelma took a deep breath. "Don't get annoyed when I say this, Audrey, but even before the fire, I noticed the Wednesday paper didn't sell half the copies of the Saturday edition."

I nodded. "I know. Go on."

"Well," Fidelma started and held up her hand in a defensive gesture. "This is just an idea, okay? I thought we might drop the Wednesday paper and just do a digital one that day, for people to check the main news and deaths and births and stuff like that and *then*, on Saturdays, do a big thing, with a weekend supplement with loads of stuff." She drew breath.

I leaned against Dan's desk. "Stuff? What kind of stuff?"

"Everything," Fidelma replied. "Cooking, gardening, fashion, sports events, interviews with interesting people, a column with country life, outdoorsy activities like hiking and riding and fishing—"

"We could have human interest stories," Mary cut in.

"And interview newcomers, especially those from foreign countries," Sinead added. "There are quite a lot of people from exotic places like Africa and the Far East around this area. Wouldn't it be great to have their stories?"

"Fantastic idea," I agreed. "There are so many immigrants here from all over the world. Their experiences of living in an Irish country town must be worth telling."

Sinead nodded, making her ponytail bob. "Yeah, they are. There's a Japanese girl next door to us. Lives with a guy from Donegal. I'd love to write her story."

I added "ethnic minorities and their stories" to the list on my tablet. "Any more ideas?"

"Photo competitions," Dan suggested.

"A health section," Mary said. "With tips from that guy at the gym. He makes these healthy smoothies, and he knows so much about diets and exercise. We could call it 'Joe's Hot Tips,' because he's…hot," she ended, her face pink.

"Holy Mother." I laughed. "You're all hopping with ideas. Keep them coming. And yes, Fidelma, I've been thinking along those lines myself. Only an online edition midweek. Could save us money, which would be funnelled into the Saturday paper and that supplement. Could be a glossy magazine that'd be on sale all week. Brilliant! But for now, let's do a nice little Wednesday paper, and then we'll announce the launch of the new weekend magazine in—how long?"

"Two weeks," Fidelma said. "If we only have three months to up the circulation, we'd better put our skates on. But I suppose you have to clear this with the publisher first?"

I sighed. "Yes. Of course. I'll send him a detailed e-mail, stressing the money-saving aspect of all of this and the potential of that weekend supplement. Fingers crossed he'll be too busy playing golf to object."

Sinead sighed. "Jesus, Mary, and Joseph, I don't envy you that task. That guy sure is hot, but I bet he's not easy to handle."

"Not for Audrey, "Dan muttered. "She has the bitchy edge."

I blinked and stared at him. "What?"

He met my stare defiantly. "Yeah, you do. You've got the power, Audrey. And it's a good thing."

"The power?" I mumbled. "You think?"

"I know it," he said with more fire in his voice than I'd ever heard before. He raised his fist in the air. "Go, Audrey!"

I laughed. "I'll probably end up backing off, but I'll put all my heart and soul into this. *The Knockmealdown News* must never die."

CHAPTER 7

My own move started later that morning when a big blue van pulled up outside the gate. My dad, in a baseball cap and sunglasses, stuck his head out of the driver's window and waved. "Hello, darlin', we're here with your furniture."

"We?" I asked, running to hug him as he got out.

"I brought two lads to help out. Paddy and Andy. They're builders. They'll have it all inside in no time at all."

Two burly young men in tee shirts and shorts alighted from the van. They smiled, nodded, and went to the back of the van to unload.

I took a look at my dad, whom I hadn't seen for at least three months. With his thick white hair and brown eyes, he was youthful and fit, with a wiry body and an impish smile that made older women weak at the knees.

"Howerya, ya old geezer?" I hugged him again.

"Fine, sweetheart." He held me at arm's length, studying me intently. "You've lost weight. You look exhausted. Are you okay?"

I pulled away. "I'm fine. The past week was a little stressful, but it seems to have sorted itself out. We were able to rent the apartment above mine on a temporary basis, so I won't have a long commute."

He smiled and patted my cheek. "Good. Let's have a look at this new place, then, so we can tell the lads where to put everything."

"Great. Can't wait to have somewhere to sit."

A few minutes later, Dad looked around the living room. "This is a grand room. You'll be happy here. I brought the blue sofa and your mum's chair and the coffee table from our family room. And all your books. Plenty of room for them in the bookcases, don't you think?"

"Absolutely."

"You've got a cat," Dad exclaimed and picked up Cat, who had escaped from the kitchen. He stroked her glossy black fur. "It's a handsome fella. What's his name?"

"It's a she, and her name's Cat."

Dad laughed and put Cat on the floor, where she weaved around the boxes, sniffing at them. "Purrfect name, I'd say. Beautiful animal."

"I love her. I hope she'll like her new home."

"With that garden? Of course she will."

We didn't have time for more chatting as "the lads" brought in load after load from the van. Dad had added a lot more than what was on my list, and I was amazed to see the things from my childhood home being carried in.

"The Indian rug from my bedroom!" I exclaimed as it was rolled out on the floor in front of the sofa. "And the lamps from your living room. Dad, you'll have nothing left."

"I'll have plenty," he said, picking a book from one of the boxes. "I'm thinking of selling the house and downsizing into something smaller, anyway. Do you want the books in alphabetical order or by author?"

"By author," I said. "But they should be in alphabetical order."

"Gotcha." He picked up another book. "I'll start with the Jane Austen collection, so."

"Hello?" a voice called from the front door. "Do you need any help?"

"We're in here, Liz," I called. "Come and meet my dad."

Dressed in a pink tee shirt, denim dungarees, and white

ballet flats, Liz looked as cute as a cupcake. I could see her face light up as she spotted Dad. She held out her hand. "Hi. I'm Liz, Audrey's new neighbour."

Dad put down the books and shook her hand, grinning broadly. "Hi, Liz. Great to meet you. My name's Sean."

I could see they clicked at once. They must be around the same age, I realised, and would probably have a lot in common. Wouldn't it be great if… But I pushed the thought away. I'd been there so many times, introducing Dad to nice women his age and only ending up disappointed. You couldn't make people fall in love, they had to do it all by themselves. In any case, he always smiled at women this way. It didn't mean he fancied them, just that he liked women in general.

"How about coffee?" Liz said. "Or a cool drink? I'm sure you'd like to take a break in this hot weather."

"Thanks, but I'm afraid I have to get back to Abbeyleix," Dad said with more than a touch of regret in his voice. "I only took a half-day from the bank. And the lads have to get back to their building site or their boss will have their blood." He looked at me. "Give me a shout if you need anything else."

I looked around at the furniture, the boxes of kitchen equipment, and the stacks of paintings and laughed. "I won't need anything else for a long time, Dad. But maybe you could come and help me put up the pictures at the weekend? And some of the curtain rails need replacing."

Dad put his arm around me. "Sure thing, girl. I'll bring my toolkit and put everything up for you on Sunday, okay?"

I agreed, and Dad and the lads were on their way back, leaving me with the boxes.

Liz looked at the departing van through the window, a dreamy expression in her eyes. "Your dad's a nice man. Very charming. Gorgeous smile."

"I know." I sighed and shook my head. "He does that to all women."

Liz's face fell. "He does?"

"Yes. It's part of his charm. He likes the company of women. But getting involved with him is a different matter. He's quite a complicated man."

"In what way?"

"He lives with a ghost. The ghost of my mother, who died when I was seven. Quite a challenge for any woman."

Liz looked suddenly uncomfortable. She put her hand on my arm. "Oh God, I'm so sorry. I had no idea. Of course that would leave a huge trauma for you both. That's the problem when you take everything at face value and try to rush into friendships. I keep doing that, and then things turn out to be more complicated under the surface."

I felt immediately sorry for Liz. Rushing into friendships was something very lonely people often did. Living on her own at her age must be so hard.

I put my hand on hers. "I'm so glad I'm going to have you for a neighbour. And if that coffee's still going, I'd love it."

Liz brightened. "It's ready in the garden. I've got some cupcakes from the bakery too."

"Now you're talking. But I'd better lock Cat in the bedroom. I don't want her to stalk the bird table. And I want to get an e-mail off to the publisher to let him know what's happening at the paper."

"Okay." Liz walked to the door. "You know where to find me."

"See you in a minute."

Liz stopped and turned. "What time on Sunday do you think your dad will be here?"

* * *

My e-mail hadn't placated Christopher one bit. He called me later that day and said we had to have a meeting.

"How about dinner here at the hotel tomorrow evening?" he suggested.

Dinner in his hotel, I thought *Wine, chat, flirting, and his bed upstairs… No, please don't go there, Audrey.* "How about lunch at the Bianconi?" I said, my voice crisp. "I'm busy in the evening." *Busy unpacking books*, I thought.

"Yeah, okay," he grunted. "We can do dinner another day."

No, we can't. "Good. One o'clock okay?"

"One thirty. I'm playing golf all morning. I'll need a shower before I meet you."

I turned my mind away from the image of his naked body in the shower. "Perfect. See you then. Bye, Christopher."

"Please, call me Kit. All my friends do."

"I'm not your friend," I said. "But okay. Bye…Kit."

"Bye, babe," he purred.

"I'm not your babe," I snapped. But he had already hung up.

* * *

My outfit for the lunch consisted of a black linen shift with a high neckline and a skirt that came to the middle of my knees. Perfectly respectable and the most boring item in my wardrobe. With ballet flats and no make-up or jewellery, it would send the right signals to Christopher: business and no shenanigans on the side.

"He won't get a chance to get flirty," I said to Cat as I gathered up my notes and phone and put them in my bag. "Strictly business."

Cat's green eyes had that "Who are you kidding?" look as I sprayed some Cristal by Chanel behind my ears and on my wrists.

"Well, I don't want to smell bad, do I?" I told her. "Even at a business meeting."

Cat turned her back on me and curled up on the sofa, to which she had taken a particular liking. She was happy in her new place. And so was I. Happy to finally be a grown-up with my own home on my own terms.

And what a gorgeous flat it was, with its spacious rooms and peaceful garden. I had spent all of the previous evening unpacking books and shoving pieces of furniture around, until they all finally found their right places: the sofa in front of the fireplace, flanked by my mother's easy chair and a leather armchair from my dad's study. The lamps with their silk shades cast pools of warm light on the Indian rug, and the full moon shone in through the tall curtainless windows. Only half the books had been placed in the bookcase, but they already gave the room that homely feel.

I had gone to bed happy, with Cat snoozing in her basket in the kitchen, guarding me from all evil. And now I was ready to fight for the newspaper that I had come to love and all the people who worked so hard for it. *Watch out, Christopher Montgomery*, I thought, *don't mess with an Irish girl on a mission.*

* * *

I marched into the dining room at the Bianconi Inn about two minutes past one and was met by a waiter who told me Mr Montgomery was waiting for me in the garden. Only slightly deflated that my grand entrance had been botched, I followed him out to the shady lawn behind the hotel, where tables had been set under the large oak trees. Christopher was sitting at a table by the fish pond looking at his phone. Dressed in white trousers and a pink shirt, his hair damp from the shower, he looked relaxed, if slightly tired. He got up as I approached and pulled out my chair.

"Hello, Audrey. Nice to see you. Would you like a drink?"

"Hello, eh, Kit." I sat down. "I'll just have water. I never drink in the middle of the day."

He gestured at his glass of cold beer. "Not even an ice-cold Carlsberg? Delicious in this heat."

"Beer makes me burp. Never touch it."

He laughed and sat down. "Yes, there is that. But I can handle it. Now, what would you like to eat?"

I picked up the menu and scanned the list. "I'll have the crab salad with some soda bread."

"Sounds nice and light." He nodded at a waiter who had just appeared, pad and pen ready to take our order. "Crab salad for the young lady and the smoked salmon on brown bread for me. Bring us a bottle of Ballygowan and another beer."

"Straight away, sir," the waiter said and walked away.

Kit put his napkin in his lap and turned to me. "So, let's talk about the plans, then. A Saturday supplement, you said in your e-mail. Some kind of magazine?"

I nodded. "Yes. We thought we'd scrap the Wednesday paper and just have an online version that day. We want to update the website to make it more like a newspaper instead of a site with different pages. A bit like *The Irish Times* layout, if you've seen their website."

"No, I haven't, but go on."

"Okay. So then the weekend edition would be the big event, so to speak. It would be a glossy magazine with lots of different sections. We'd have food, health, fitness, gardening, fashion…" I paused. Why was he staring at me? "And we'd also cover more serious things, such as local politics and immigration and social affairs. Homelessness and so on." I drew breath.

Kit said nothing while we were served our meal. He drank some beer. Picked up his knife and fork and put them down again. "Well," he started, "that's a very ambitious plan. How much is all this going to cost?"

I pulled a sheet of paper from my bag. "Mary has worked

out a plan. We think we can save money by not having a print version on Wednesday, which also cuts down on the money we spend on distribution."

"If you all took a pay cut, that would also help," Kit interrupted, merely glancing at my page.

I stared at him. "Pay cut? We're working for peanuts as it is. We haven't had a raise since you bought the paper three years ago. What do you think we are? A Chinese sweatshop?"

He laughed. "Oh come on, it's not that bad."

"No, but if we don't get a raise soon, the girls will leave. We have a great team there, you know. Excellent staff who will work their guts out for our paper. "

He picked up his knife and fork again. "Please, calm down. I was joking. I love it when your eyes flash like that."

I looked down at my crab salad, willing myself to stay calm. Then I looked up and met his teasing eyes. "I'd be grateful if you could keep to business and hold the personal remarks."

He put his hand on mine. "That, my darling, is going to be very difficult. You're a beautiful, intelligent woman with a feisty spirit. That's an irresistible combination. You can come here and wear no make-up and that nun's dress and the flat shoes, but it only makes you even more desirable. Forgive me if I stray from the professional path from time to time, but you're too much of a distraction. You can't deny there is a certain, eh, chemistry between us."

"No," I mumbled, his touch nearly paralysing me. "But that shouldn't impact on our professional relationship."

He removed his hand. "I'll do my best to act correctly, that's all I can promise."

Recovering my cool, I looked back at him. "Kit, I will never succumb to your undeniable charms. You're my boss. I have my own rules about that kind of relationship. I'll never sleep with you. That's final." I drew breath.

He was silent for a long time. Then he took a long pull of

his beer. "What if I fired you? Then I wouldn't be your boss."

"Then I'd hate you forever."

"No, you wouldn't. You'd finally give in. I can see it in your eyes."

I gritted my teeth. "Listen, I didn't come here to play games with you. If you're not going to be adult enough to discuss my plan for the paper, I'll go back to the office and we'll work to the original deal. We'll get the circulation back to what it was and stick to your deal or ultimatum or whatever the feck you want to call it."

Kit laughed and held up his hands. "Okay, settle down. Let's be professional, then and enjoy our lunch."

"Thank you." I picked up my knife and fork, and we ate in silence for a while, until Kit wiped his mouth and cleared his throat.

"So," he started, "I've been considering your plan. It's good, but there's no proof it won't end up costing money if the sales don't take off at once. But you can go ahead on the same condition as before: You have three months to get it off the ground. After that, the gloves are off. If we lose money, the paper is history. Got that?"

I nodded and put my napkin on the table. "Got it. I take it nobody gets a raise?"

"Not at the moment. We'll revise the salaries at the end of the three-month period."

"Right." I got up. "Thanks for lunch. I'll be in touch. By e-mail."

He rose. "Look, Audrey, I like you. A lot. I don't mean it in a sexist way at all when I say this. I admire your strength, your way with people, and your tremendous guts. But what you're doing here in this little town running a local newspaper is a mystery to me. You could have a much higher profile in Dublin or even London. We're looking for an editor for our new project over there. If you're interested, I'll e-mail you the details. Could be a great new start for you. More money, and a new career in journalism. What do you say?"

We looked at each other across the table while his words sank in. Did he mean it? Probably not. But the idea tickled my senses. A high-profile job in London? My dad would be so proud. But… "Thank you, Kit," I said. "That's very nice to hear, of course. But I'm happy here. I'm a country girl at heart. And *The Knockmealdown News* is my baby. I want to see it grow up."

He smiled and shook his head. "You're a strange girl, Audrey. Not many women would refuse an offer like this. But, strange as it may seem, I understand where you're coming from. This is a nice town, a nice place to live. I envy you in a way, if you see what I mean. Being part of a community like this is probably better than any glitzy London life. Not that I'd want to change mine for this, but I do understand." He held out his hand. "Can we be friends?"

I shook his hand. "Not sure about the friends bit, but thanks. Bye for now, Kit." I dropped his hand and walked away, feeling as if I'd just been on a roller coaster ride. But I left the restaurant with a completely different opinion of Christopher Montgomery than when I had arrived.

CHAPTER 8

The following Sunday, with the plans for the new weekend edition coming along nicely, I took a break from work to spend time with my dad. He arrived bright and early in his old Volvo loaded with tools. It was yet another hot day of the freak Mediterranean summer we were having. Knowing he would have rushed over without eating, I had laid out a breakfast of scrambled eggs, sausages, and brown bread on the old table in the garden. Cat walked around in the dappled sunlight under the old rose bushes, pouncing on ants and the odd grasshopper. I could hear music coming from the other side of the wall. Liz was enjoying the summer as much as I was.

Dad dropped his toolbox on the floor of the living room when he spotted the food through the open window. "You made me breakfast."

"I knew you wouldn't have bothered eating."

Dad went into the garden and sat down on one of the rickety chairs but hopped up again. "This chair's wobbly. Let me just…" He ran to get a wrench from his toolbox and tightened the screws on the chair before he sat down again. "There. Should be safe now. But you should fix the other ones and oil them. This is hardwood. Needs to be oiled regularly."

"I know." I sighed. "I'll do it as soon as things calm down a bit. I'll get the tea."

"Thanks." Dad dug into the spread before him. He was about to bite into one of the sausages, but his fork froze in mid-air. "That music. Where is it coming from?"

"The garden next door. It belongs to Liz. You know, the cute woman you met last Tuesday."

"Oh." He put the sausage into his mouth and chewed while he listened. "It's Seán Ó Riada. 'The Banks of Sulán.' Beautiful." His eyes had a distant look as he ate, listening to the lilting tune, so fitting for a warm Sunday morning in June. How strange that Liz should be playing that particular piece by that particular composer just then.

The morning quickly turned busy and noisy with Dad hammering and banging, hanging pictures and curtain rails, putting together the bedroom furniture from IKEA, and readjusting some of the kitchen cupboards he declared were in danger of falling down. I was holding the ladder as he was putting up the light fixture in the living room ceiling when the door opened and Liz peered in, Jonathan hovering behind her.

"Hello?" she called. "Can we come in? We're bearing gifts and food." I noticed she hadn't taken a huge amount of trouble dressing up, but she still looked nice in her white shirt and jeans. Fresh and classy with a slight tan. Cool and unassuming. "I hope we're not interrupting," she added cautiously.

Dad laughed and came down the ladder. "All done. Hello there…Liz?"

Liz laughed and came in. "That's right. And you're Sean. I was playing some music by your namesake earlier. I hope it didn't disturb you."

Dad beamed. "Not at all. It was a lovely surprise. Ó Riada happens to be one of my favourite composers."

Liz returned his smile. "How odd. Not many people seem to like him. But I do. He had that Celtic soul, don't you think? As if his music rose from the Irish soil."

"That's a lovely image." Dad looked past Liz. "And is this your son?"

Jonathan laughed. "No, I'm Jonathan O'Regan. The owner of the building." He held out his hand. "And also, I hope, a friend of Audrey. Nice to meet you, Mr Killian."

"Please. Call me Sean. I'm not a hundred years old yet."

They shook hands, then Liz revealed the contents of her basket, and Jonathan pulled a bottle of chilled wine from the bag he carried. "A housewarming gift that I was hoping we could all share."

With much laughing and joking, we went out to the garden and sat down on the grass after I had found wine-glasses and plates in one of the boxes under the kitchen table. Liz had made a chicken salad and bought two baguettes at the bakery down the street, with an apple pie to finish. There was more than enough for everyone, including Cat, who gobbled up the piece of chicken Liz put on the grass for her.

Jonathan and I tidied up and made coffee while Dad and Liz continued to chat. Jonathan filled the sink with hot water and detergent. "We might as well wash up while they're getting to know each other."

I grabbed a towel from the hook by the sink. "Yes, they're getting on well."

"A budding romance?"

I shook my head and sighed. "I wish. But no, don't think so. Dad is still living in the past. He says Mum's waiting for him in the next life. I have a feeling he doesn't really want another woman in his life. He's quite content on his own. Loves music and reading and fixing things. And now he says he's moving out of his house when he retires from the bank at the end of the year. I bet he'll buy an old wreck that'll take years to do up. Just his cup of tea."

Jonathan turned and looked at me. "And you? How are you settling in?"

"So far I love it. The office upstairs is a little small for what we plan to do, but it's fine until we have the new weekend edition off the ground. Then we'll show the publisher it'll be a huge success. It has to be or…"

"Or…?"

"We're all out on the street looking for a job."

Jonathan put a plate in the rack. "Can he do that?"

I sighed. "Of course he can. He's the publisher."

"Who is he?" Jonathan asked, rinsing the glasses.

"Christopher Montgomery of the Montgomery Group. They own a huge number of newspapers and magazines all over Britain and Ireland."

"Like a small-town Murdoch or something?"

I dried the glasses and put them in a cupboard. "Yes. Something like that. And he throws his weight around in a similar fashion. I used to hate him. But I've discovered he's not all that bad. Fancies himself too much of course and has an irritating attitude toward women."

"But he has a nice side too?" Jonathan looked at me while the water gurgled in the pipes as he pulled the plug.

"Let's call it a 'not-as-bad-as-he-looks' side."

"Or 'I-fancy-him' wishful thinking?"

I dried the cutlery and put it in a drawer before I replied. Then I met Jonathan's eyes. "Okay, I admit it. I fancy him. And maybe I'm hoping he's better than he looks. But he's my boss, so that's a one-way street I'll never turn into."

Jonathan leaned against the sink and folded his arms. "Why do you fancy him?"

I sighed. "I don't know. His bedroom eyes? The way he looks at me? The way my whole body tingles at even the slightest physical contact? I'm ashamed of myself, to be honest, but I can't help feeling drawn to him. He's an intelligent man but ruthless. Maybe I want to sleep with him and then kick him in the balls?" I put my hands over my face. "I must be mad. What's wrong with me?"

"Nothing at all." Jonathan put his arms around me.

"You're confused. You want to be the cool editor, the career woman without feelings. But then your heart and your hormones get in the way. Don't worry about it. Stay strong and follow your own star."

I hugged him back and put my head on his chest. "My star," I mumbled against his crisp linen shirt. "I'd follow it if I could find it."

He hugged me tighter. "You'll find it. But stay cool and don't get involved with that man. He'll only break your heart."

I pulled away and gave him a wobbly smile. "You're right. You're a wonderful friend, Jonathan. Thanks for listening."

He put his hand on my arm. "Audrey, I'll always be here for you. I know we've only just met, but if you need a friend, you know where I am."

"You're a brick, Jonathan. Now let's make coffee to go with the apple pie."

"Yeah, I'm a brick. As solid as the wall." He shook himself. "But go on, let's make coffee and enjoy the lovely day." There was a sad twist to his smile that puzzled me. Maybe he was also lost and lonely, looking for love? If he weren't gay, he'd be any girl's dream. Even mine.

* * *

Kit called me later that evening. "Are you in bed?"

I turned off the TV. "No. It's only ten thirty. I've just watched the BBC news. What do you want?"

"That, my dear girl, is not something I wish to tell you. But here's an idea I had. Why not do a launch for the new magazine?"

I sat up. "You're going to host it at Killybeg? Why don't you ask Pandora to organise it?"

He laughed softly. "Gosh, no. That wouldn't go down well

with the locals. I was thinking something rural and home-spun. A party at that old pub in the middle of town. What's it called? McKenna's?"

"McCarthy's," I corrected.

"That's it. We could do country music, pints of Guinness, and that vile Irish food that's so popular around here."

"I don't think that's a good idea."

"Why?"

"It just isn't. It'll cost money, and it would only attract people who'd come for a free drink. Forget it, Kit. There's going to be a staff party, though. I just spoke to Jerry's sister-in-law, Jules. She's throwing us a party on Saturday night at her house, just the staff and a few friends. You'd be welcome too, of course," I said without thinking.

"Uh, okay. Thanks. I'll think about it."

"How long are you planning to stay here?"

"Oh," he said airily, "I haven't decided yet. But at least another week. There are some rather spiffing people from Dublin at the hotel right now."

"Oh, uh, that's good." I managed not to laugh at the use of "spiffing." So very posh boarding school. "Let me know about Saturday night."

"Right-oh. Talk to you soon. Good luck with the maga-zine. Looking forward to seeing the first issue."

Me too, I thought when he had hung up. It was all a bit of a mess, trying to decide on a theme and a new look for the cover. It had to be perfect right from the start. But the articles were shaping up nicely. We were doing a "hero of the week" spot where we'd feature young people who had done something amazing, be it in sports, academics, or cultural pursuits such as Irish dancing or music. Then my own favourite: an interview with a newcomer from a foreign country. As there had been a big influx of refugees and other foreign nationals to rural Ireland, it was important to write their stories. It would make Irish people more inclined to see foreigners as a welcome part of the community who would add colour and new life to small towns such as ours. Many Irish people still clung to old traditions and were suspicious of outsiders. Even I was seen as a blow-in, and that kind of thinking had to be stamped out.

I called Cat in from the garden, closed the windows, and turned out the lights. I was about to get into bed when the phone rang.

It was Jules. "Just to check you're all right there all on your own."

"I'm fine." I sat down on the bed. "Why wouldn't I be? I love my new flat. It's the first time in my life I've had my own home. I always lived with other people before or in someone's guest room."

"About time you had your own place, then. But I—or Marcus, to be exact—thought I should call and check to see if you were all right."

Marcus. I closed my eyes for a moment. We'd had a fling that had seemed casual at the time, but there were both lingering regret and tenderness between us. It could have been so great if only... "You can tell him I'm absolutely delighted with my flat. Never felt more content, actually. The neighbours are terrific too. Lovely woman next door. And Jonathan O'Regan, the historian, upstairs. So I really fell on my feet when this flat came up."

"Marcus told the agency about you. They were about to call you when you beat them to it."

"He did? Well, there was no need. I would have found it all on my own."

"I know. Anyway, if you need anything, give us a shout. And we'll see you at the party on Saturday."

"Oh." A thought struck me. "I invited the publisher too, hope you don't mind."

"Of course not. Should be fun to meet him. And how about inviting your neighbours? That nice woman. And

Jonathan O'Regan? I've seen his TV programme about the Iron Age finds. I'd love to meet him in person. I could listen to him speak for hours."

"Yes, me too. He has a wonderful voice. Sounds boring, but he's a very interesting man."

"Cute too," Jules chortled.

"Very," I agreed. "Pity he's gay. But in a way that's a good thing. We're becoming close friends."

"He's gay?" Jules said incredulously. "That's news to me. I mean, it's never been mentioned anywhere."

"Maybe he's keeping it quiet? After all, that's nobody's business, is it?"

"Except his ex-girlfriend's?"

I froze. "What?"

"He used to date a TV producer. A nice woman called Anne-Marie. Tall brunette. I've seen pictures of them in gossip magazines at the dentists'. Years out of date of course. The magazines, I mean."

"Jonathan and a woman? Are you sure it was him?"

"Positive. There couldn't be another historian with the same name. But they broke up. I think she married someone else, in any case."

I was speechless. Jonathan wasn't gay? But Liz had said— What had she said exactly? That Jonathan was "close to his feminine side," which I took to mean— Which it didn't. He wasn't really gay. And I'd been pouring my heart out to him about my sex life and all kinds of other personal details. How embarrassing.

"Audrey?" Jules called at the other end. "You still there?"

"Yes," I mumbled. "Just a little confused."

"About Jonathan? Well, you know what? Maybe he discovered he was gay, and that's why he broke up with her. I mean, there has been no woman since, as far as I know."

I thought for a moment. "That's possible, of course. In fact it seems the most likely situation. We've become quite close in a very short time but not close enough for him to talk about that kind of thing."

"Is this a problem for you?"

"Not really. I like him a lot. He's a terrific friend."

"Isn't that enough for now?" Jules asked. "Isn't it better to just go with the flow and enjoy the friendship?"

I considered this for a moment and realised she was right.

"Hello?" Jules called. "You still there?"

"Yes. Sorry. A bit tired. We're working so hard on the new magazine."

"Of course," Jules soothed. "I'll let you go. We'll call around some evening to inspect the new flat."

She said goodnight, and I hung up, my head spinning. Was Jules right? Or was Jonathan not gay at all? But maybe he and that woman had just been friends, with a relationship similar to ours. He hadn't talked about his love life during that long warm evening on the terrace. But I hadn't given him a chance as I rambled on about my own woes. He had listened and been so sympathetic and supportive but never once opened his mouth about any of his own troubles. What was going on behind that sweet expression? And what about Kit? He was showing a nice side I found hard to believe. And then Marcus being so concerned about me. I felt the beginnings of a headache. Things were getting seriously complicated.

CHAPTER 9

The first issue of the weekend magazine was in the shops on the appointed Saturday in mid-June. I got up at seven and rushed to the nearest newsagent. I was thrilled to see it there on the counter. The new logo and the typeface were a little old-fashioned, but they suited our style perfectly. It was simply called *Country Weekend*, since we hadn't come up with anything catchy. But as I looked at it, I realised it didn't need anything else. No use pretending it was *Rolling Stone* or something.

I picked up a copy and tossed my four euros at the shop-keeper. "What do you think?" I asked him.

"It's going to be a real winner," he replied and pulled a copy from under the counter. "I'm reading mine right now. The story about the Japanese ballet dancer is amazing. And I liked the pub crawl feature. That's a hoot."

I laughed. "Yeah. That was Dan's idea. And the fake selfies too. He wanted something for the lads."

"My wife says doing the cookery section as a mini-magazine that you can pull out is fantastic. Then you can save them all and make your own cookery book."

I nodded and opened the magazine. "Yes, we thought that would go down well."

"Your column is a hoot. Especially the photo."

I scanned the first page and gasped. My photo beside

the letter from the editor was not the one I had picked. Dan must have made a mistake. I looked in horror at the photo of me licking ice cream from a dripping cone, my face shiny and my hair a mess. "Jaysus, I'll kill him," I muttered and raced out of the shop.

Minutes later, I was in the office. I threw the magazine on Dan's desk. "What the *hell* is this?"

He looked up from his laptop. "The magazine? Great, isn't it?"

"Yeah, except that photo is a fucking disgrace. How on earth could you have made that mistake? I thought we had agreed—"

Dan glanced at the photo and let out a snort.

"It's not funny."

He looked up at me. "Yes it is. It shows you as a normal woman, not the glamorous editor. I'm sorry I went behind your back, but we all thought it was a good idea." He tapped the photo with his finger. "Here, you look young, a little sweaty, and cute. You're struggling with the heat, just like we all are. And that's what you say in your piece too. You talk about how fecking hot it is and how we don't know how to cope with tropical weather in Ireland. 'Finally, we get to say *mañana* and mean it,' you say. The article is funny, so I thought the photo should be too." He drew breath and looked at me defiantly.

I glanced at the photo again. Then at the headline. He was right. Had it been someone else in that photo, I'd have agreed with everything he said. But it was *me* looking sweaty and messy. "Yeah, well…" I started.

"You're not brave enough to own that photo?" he asked innocently. I knew he was giving me back for all the jibes about his weight.

I stared back at him, an idea forming in my mind. "Okay. I agree. It's funny. And here's another suggestion: How about doing a weight loss feature? Like a challenge? I know you want to lose weight, so how about doing it publicly? How about we do something like *Operation Transformation*, you know, from TV last spring? Call it something else and invite others to join in? Put up candid shots of you and then every week do a weigh-in and make that part of the health section?"

Dan's chubby face turned red. "That would be hard for me. Not sure I can do that, to be honest."

"If you do it, I'll agree to a candid shot of me beside my piece every week. I'll make an eejit of myself on purpose to go with whatever article I write. I had planned to make every editorial funny anyway. They're usually so boring. I'll give you the right to take any shot of me at an unguarded moment and publish it."

Dan swallowed. Then he nodded. "Okay. If you agree to that, I'll do it. I'll talk to Mary about it since she handles the health section. I'll get some of the lads in the pub to join me. Maybe this time I'll finally nail this weight loss thing."

I squeezed his shoulder. "That's my boy. You *will* do it. You will, you will, you will. And now I'll make us both a cup of tea, and then we'll thrash around this new idea when the girls get here. Wasn't it lucky you came in early?"

"I wouldn't call it lucky," he muttered.

* * *

I arrived at Knocknagow House a little ahead of time. I hadn't been to Jules' house since Marcus moved in. Surprised, I looked at the well-tended lawns, the new tubs of roses, and the fresh gravel on the path leading to the front entrance. The steps had been repaired and the massive front door repainted a dark red. I pulled the chain for the bell, just to see if that too had been fixed. I was met by a loud chiming inside. Then the door flew open, and I was welcomed not by

Jules but by her sister Dessie, beaming me a huge grin.

"Audrey," she squealed and threw her arms around me in a hug made a little awkward by a very pregnant tummy. "Sorry, can't hug you tighter. The baby's in the way."

I pulled back and took her hands, looking at her face, shining with happiness. "Dessie, how lovely to see you. I didn't know you were home. And you're pregnant. Congratulations."

"Thank you. I'm as surprised as you are, but Rory thought I'd like to get home for a bit to get some rest. England's even hotter than here right now. In any case, we decided that he should be born in Ireland, now that the UK has decided to leave the EU, so I'm here until it's time to push."

"When's that, then?"

"August. So Jules and Marcus will have to put up with me all summer long. Rory will be here in late July too." She peered behind me. "But I thought you were bringing a date? Your landlord or something?"

"Not a date exactly. Jonathan and I are...friends. He'll be here in a minute. He wanted to have a look at the ruin on the hill. He's a historian. Can't resist old stones."

"Oh. Okay," Dessie said and winked. "None of my beeswax, right?"

"Well..." Did she notice the slight hesitation in my voice? My relationship with Jonathan hadn't changed, except for what was going on in my mind. I still had no idea if what Jules had said was true. I had no way of finding out and, in a way, I didn't want to. Whether Jonathan was gay or not was of little importance, I had decided. We were becoming close friends, which made me happy. There was no sexual tension between us—or any other kind of tension—just this calm, serene feeling of complete understanding. "I'd tell you if there were anything to tell, but there isn't," I ended.

Dessie waved her hand in the air. "Whatever will be, will be, as my granny used to say. Leave things alone and enjoy the moment. Easy to say, hard to do." She opened the door wider. "But what are we doing standing here? Come in. I bet you've never gone through the front door of this house."

I stepped into the large entrance hall. "No, I haven't. We always used to come in the back way to the kitchen." I looked around at the flagged floor and the newly painted walls hung with old oil paintings of romantic landscapes and hunting scenes. "This is lovely. Jules has worked hard."

"Not Jules, Marcus. He's done an amazing job. He managed to sell off some of the more valuable paintings to raise money for the repairs and restorations. But it didn't stretch to central heating, more's the pity. So they still live in the kitchen in the winter. But this house comes to life in the summer. Isn't it fabulous?"

"Wonderful."

"But come in. I'll leave the door open for your Jonathan whenever he's finished inspecting the ruin. Where's your bag? I heard you're staying here tonight."

"Jonathan will bring it in later."

"Okay. Come this way."

I followed Dessie through the inner hall into the drawing room, which had also been freshened up. The frayed velvet curtains had been replaced by bright chintz, matching the chairs and sofas, and the faded carpet had been cleaned. The French windows were open to the garden, where I spotted Jules at the barbecue. Her dogs lay in the grass under the trees, their tongues lolling, and Miranda was putting a big bowl of salad on a trestle table in the shade of the willow tree.

I waved at them. "Hi! What a gorgeous evening."

We greeted each other and fell into our usual banter. The three of us had been friends ever since I arrived in town. The only discord was Marcus and Jules. I had no right to even think that Jules had stolen Marcus from me, as we had broken up after a spectacular row weeks before they even started dating. Not her fault, or Marcus'. But still… I had hoped he'd come crawling back or that we would in some way kiss and make up. But too much had been said, too many insults had been thrown. There was so much pain afterwards that could never be healed with soothing words or apologies.

Marcus had said he could forgive but never forget. I suppose he felt he couldn't live with someone like me. I was too headstrong, too opinionated, and too independent. Jules wasn't a shrinking violet, but she was more the submissive, caring-for-my-man kind of female. And they shared that obsession with dogs and horses.

A match made in heaven, I thought bitterly as I watched Marcus come through the door of the conservatory with bottles of wine, giving Jules a peck on the cheek as he passed her. He stopped dead as he saw me.

"Audrey. Hello." He would have dropped all the bottles if Miranda hadn't rushed to catch them.

"Hi, Marcus." I made my hips wiggle as I walked toward him, knowing the skirt of my blue summer dress danced around my tanned legs. When I reached him, I kissed his cheek, pressing my chest into his blue cotton shirt, and whispered, "You look good enough to eat" into his ear, leaving a lipstick smear. I knew it was a tarty thing to do, and it wasn't meant as a come-on or an attempt to steal him away from Jules. I just wanted him to feel a tiny flicker of regret about what he could have had.

I could see that flicker in his eyes as our eyes met, before he broke away and shot me that wide grin I used to love. "Happy to see you too, Audrey. You look smashing tonight. Doesn't she, Jules?" he called across the lawn.

"Fecking fabulous," Jules agreed. "And we all hate her. But enough about you, what about the new magazine, then? I love it. Well done, Audrey."

"Not all my own work," I protested. "The team did an outstanding job. I think it'll go well."

"It's a hit already," Marcus said. "It was sold out at our newsagents. Great mix of frivolous, domestic, and serious. I think that 'My Journey' series will send out a powerful message and make people around here understand that immigrants are a positive thing for a community. It makes them real people, not just statistics or blow-ins who aren't welcome. Admirable, my friend."

I bobbed a mock curtsey. "Thank you, dear sir."

"Come here and help me get this bloody thing to light, willya, Marcus?" Jules interrupted. "Barbecues are men's work after all."

"Yes, my darling," he ran to her side after giving my shoulder a squeeze. "See you later, old girl. Must obey orders from the hostess."

Miranda handed me a glass of wine. "Let's have a drink while we wait for the burnt offerings. Marcus always gets it wrong. He's great in the kitchen but hasn't got the hang of the barbecue yet."

"I never will," Marcus shot back. "Never understood this taste for charred sausages you all have around here. But hey, if that's what you want, I'm your servant."

"Servant, my eye," Miranda muttered. "He wears the pants in that relationship. Never saw Jules lie down and play dead like this before. Must be true love."

"Or true lust?" I muttered, watching Marcus nibble Jules' earlobe.

"Could be," Miranda said. "But I have always believed that when you truly love someone, you have to give up a little piece of yourself. Otherwise it's just selfish, and it won't work in the long run."

"Hmm. I've never thought of it that way, but maybe you're right."

"I'm always right." Miranda smirked. "But what about that magazine, then? I have to join in with Jules and Marcus. It's remarkable for a first issue."

"Thank you. And yes, I agree. We're all very proud. Hope the boss likes it too. He said he might pop over later."

"That'd be great." Miranda looked over my shoulder. "But who's this arriving? Do I spot a minor celebrity and a fine-looking older woman? Are they a couple?"

I followed her gaze and saw Liz and Jonathan coming around the house together. "No. They're my neighbours. Liz Mulcahy and Jonathan O'Regan, the historian. Liz lives in the flat next to mine and Jonathan's upstairs. He owns the building, so that makes him my landlord. But we're also good friends."

"You lucky thing." Miranda sighed. "I *adore* Jonathan O'Regan. I wish they'd put him on TV every night. I find his voice so soothing. And he has this incredible talent to make anything interesting."

"I know. And he's very nice. Sounds boring, but I love men who're polite and considerate. You don't meet them very often."

"Great dresser too." Miranda smiled at Jonathan and held out her hand. "Hello, Jonathan, I'm Miranda, Jules' sister and Jerry Murphy's wife."

Jonathan, looking dapper in white shorts and a tight-fitting navy polo shirt, shook Miranda's hand. "Hello, Miranda. But you must be something more than a sister and wife. You look like you could be—" he stepped back and studied her "—something to do with flowers and plants? Gardens? Or orchards? That flowing dress with tiny pink roses and your long hair tells me you're close to nature."

Miranda laughed. "You must be psychic. I run an organic farm. Fruit and veg, and herbs too."

"I'm not psychic," Jonathan said. "I have to confess that I met your husband a while back, when he had that publishing house. They published my book on archaeological finds in West Cork. He told me about your farm."

"Not psychic, but honest. Much better." Miranda said.

She turned to Liz. "Sorry, didn't mean to be rude. Hello, Liz, and welcome."

Liz nodded and laughed. "No problem. I was busy admiring the garden. I love these Georgian houses with the old trees and walls. And the view of the mountains is fantastic from here."

"Bloody hell," Marcus muttered, still trying to light the charcoal under the grill of the barbecue. "We'll be eating at midnight at this rate."

Jonathan stepped forward. "Can I give you a hand with that? I do barbecues all the time, and I see yours is no different. A bit tricky, but…" He laughed. "Sorry, you don't know me at all. I'm Audrey's landlord. Jonathan O'Regan."

"Marcus Smythe. Forgive me for not shaking hands, but I'm filthy. If you can do anything with this, I'd be very grateful."

"No problem." Jonathan took the matches and the tongs from Marcus. "Let's check if the vent underneath is open. Aha, it's not. That's why it won't light. Then you have to pile up the charcoal into a pyramid like this, then sprinkle on a tiny bit of lighter fuel, and apply the match…" Jonathan worked as he talked, and soon flames started to flicker and a tiny column of smoke rose from the barbecue. "There you go. Let the flames die out, and then wait until the briquettes turn white before you put meat on top. Takes about twenty minutes."

"Excellent." Marcus clapped Jonathan on the back. "Thanks, old chap. You've saved us from starvation."

I looked at the two of them and realised how alike they were. Even though Marcus was the epitome of the English toff, and Jonathan the quirky Irishman, they had the same kindly expression and honest eyes. Neither of them would ever let you down, neither of them would ever tell lies or cheat on you. And neither of them would ever disrespect a woman. Quite unlike the man who had just arrived, who always managed to confuse and attract me, despite my efforts to reject him.

CHAPTER 10

I was still looking at Marcus, only half-listening to the conversation, when someone placed a light kiss on my bare shoulder. "Hello, lovely. Sorry I'm late." I jumped and pulled away from Kit, all dressed up in beige chinos and a navy blazer, holding a magnum of champagne in each hand. "Where do I put these?" he asked. "They need to be chilled."

"I'll see if any of the staff are around," I said with just a hint of sarcasm. "Or maybe the butler can help you."

"There's a butler?" Kit looked around. "I don't see any—" He stopped. "Oh yeah, I get it. You're having me on."

"Big time, sweetie," I chortled. "So, what did you think of the magazine, then? What's the verdict?"

Kit looked only slightly embarrassed. "Uh, well, I haven't had a chance…"

I glared at him. "Shit, you didn't bother to read it."

"I will. Later. Promise." He pushed the bottles at me. "What'll I do with these?"

I took the bottles. "I'll put them in the freezer for a bit. You go and introduce yourself. The cute woman with short blonde hair is Jules, the tall brunette in hippie clothing is her sister Miranda, and the gorgeous pregnant woman is the third sister, Dessie. The hunk trying to light the barbecue is Jules' boyfriend, Marcus, and the mature but very beautiful female in the pink dungarees is my neighbour, Liz."

"Who's the overgrown boy scout?"

I bristled at his sneery tone. "That's Jonathan. He's actually the most interesting man here."

"Sounds very charming." Kit moved closer. "I'll go and meet them all. Will we get together later? Under the trees over there to look at the stars?"

"In your dreams," was all I managed before he galloped down the slope and greeted everyone as if he'd known them for years. Even more annoying was him acting as if we were a couple. But when I saw Marcus' puzzled eyes, I decided to play along. Why not let them all think Kit and I were an item, especially Marcus?

I went to the kitchen to put the two magnums in the tall freezer, reminding myself not to forget to take them out before they froze. I crammed the bottles in between two huge bags of frozen vegetables and slammed the door shut, just as Jonathan walked in.

"Do you know where the meat for the barbecue is?" he enquired. "Jules asked me to get it. She said it was in the kitchen."

"There." I pointed at the steaks on a wooden board on top of the freezer. "Out of reach of the dogs."

"Thanks. They'll need them in about twenty minutes, when the barbecue's hot enough."

I dragged a tall stool to the freezer. "I'll get them for you."

Without waiting for a reply, I kicked off my sandals and got up on the stool, realising too late I was giving Jonathan a great view of my knickers. He glanced up and immediately turned his gaze away, but not before I saw the glint of something close to lust in those hazel eyes. Moments later, as I handed him the steaks, I was sure I had imagined that brief flash. I had been overthinking his feelings for me as I wrestled with all that stuff Jules had told me. "Shut up," I said to myself.

"What?" Jonathan asked, looking alarmed.

"Nothing." I laughed. "I thought I heard the dogs barking." I jumped down from the stool. "It's the heat. Makes you kind of crazy sometimes."

"Not me. Just makes me sleepy. Not a huge help when I have a deadline for that paper I'm writing for the university." He stood there, holding the steaks, looking at me. "You know what?"

"What?" I couldn't help smiling at his sweet expression and earnest eyes.

"Your magazine. It's really good. I read all of it this morning in one go, sitting on my terrace. Should have been writing, but I got so caught up in the articles. And as I read it, I felt there was something missing."

"Missing? Like what?"

"An historical feature. I mean, our town and all this area are steeped in history. From megalithic tombs to Norman castles and everything in between and beyond, all the way to modern times, there is so much to discover and learn. Most people don't bother. But it's part of our heritage and who we are." He drew breath, looking at me with something akin to passion.

"Hmm." I thought for a while. "I'm not sure I want to do that. I feel we need to sex it up a bit, not be all intellectual or housewifely all the time." An idea suddenly hit me. "How about combining sex and history? 'Scandal of the Week' or something? I mean," I babbled as Jonathan looked alarmed. "We could have an historical scandals page. You know, those illicit love affairs from long ago. I'm sure we could find some saucy stuff if we looked hard enough. That would be both informative and fun. It'd make people learn history while thinking they're reading something kinky. Teaching history by stealth. How about that?"

As Jonathan considered my idea, a slow smile in his eyes turned into a cheeky grin. "Sex and history? Perfect. There're quite a few old scandals in the archives of the castle, for example. Then we have nuns and priests and the reported secret tunnels between the convent and the abbey…" He nodded. "Yeah. Let's do it."

"There should be images. Perhaps old portraits?"

He nodded. "Yes. There are lots we could use. I even have some in my computer files."

"We could call it 'Fifty Shades of History,'" I suggested with a wink.

Jonathan laughed. "You're a scream, Audrey." He glanced at the board with the steaks he was holding. "But let's go and cook up a storm. Everyone must be starving."

I opened the freezer and fished out the two magnums of champagne. "I think these are chilled enough."

"Must be. We've been here about half an hour."

We went to join the party and found that everyone from the office had just arrived. Mary, Fidelma, and Sinead, all dressed up, and Dan with a diminutive brunette called Sally, who he told me was his girlfriend. We opened the champagne, the steaks were cooked to perfection by Jonathan, and Marcus was happily mixing salad and cutting up bread. "Much less risky," he declared. "Thanks for inviting the chef of the year, Audrey," he said without the slightest hint of embarrassment.

The girls flocked around Kit and expressed their thanks for giving us the money to do the magazine and rescue the paper. He lapped it all up, flirting with them all in his slightly lewd way, which got heavier the more champagne he drank. I was going to get Mary away from him when I saw him sliding his hand down her back to her bottom, but she said something under her breath and stepped away smartly, leaving him looking foolish. *Good on you, Mary. You can look after yourself*, I thought and shot her a smile.

"Are all Irish birds this bitchy?" Kit asked, pulling me aside. "Or is it only around here?"

"It's quite widespread throughout the country," I said. "Us

Celtic chicks like to be handled with courtesy and respect."

He nodded and lifted his glass, which Jules had just topped up. "Cheers to them. I like girls with a bit of sass. But you're the belle of the ball tonight, lovely."

I couldn't help laughing. I felt as light as air, the champagne and the new plans I had made with Jonathan lifting my spirits. Combined with the beautiful evening, the setting sun behind the Galtee Mountains in the west leaving a pink tinge to the darkening sky, I felt as if I could fly.

I lifted my own glass. "Cheers, Kit. To our new venture, even if you couldn't be arsed to look at it yet. And cheers to a new item I have just discussed with our new collaborator."

He looked startled. "New venture? Collaborator? Is this going to cost me even more money?"

I smiled and winked. "No, darlin', it will *make* you money in the end. And, as it's kind of suggestive, it'll be something you'll love."

He looked doubtful. "I smell a conspiracy. You're doing something behind my back and flirting with me to cover it up." He moved closer, sliding his arm around my waist. "But I'll play along for now."

I leaned against him, sipping champagne, looking at the view. Funny, I didn't really like him, but it felt good to be so close. Somehow, he managed to move us further away, to a spot behind the trees that was more private. I didn't protest. His hand on my waist gave me a faint tingle, and his lips brushing my neck wasn't off-putting in the slightest, quite the opposite. It was just a physical attraction, and a little voice deep down whispered, "Don't," but I ignored it and turned to him as he put both his arms around me and looked deep into my eyes.

"You're a very sexy woman," he said, his lips brushing mine. "Very desirable."

"Mmm. You too." I lifted my glass behind his back and took a sip behind his shoulder. Then I met his hot eyes and fell into some kind of deep hole of desire while we kissed.

Oh God, could that man kiss. Long, deep, sensual, his tongue probing, his hands on my back, seeking my bare skin above the dress. His firm body, his muscular thighs, and then his erection pushing at my groin. The champagne, the warm air, the moon rising, that magic of the summer night all made my head swim and my body respond shamelessly. My glass fell with a tinkle to the grass, but I was unable to break away to pick it up. I was hypnotised, my sensuality surging to the surface as he kept kissing me and touching me in the light of the rising moon. The background sound of laughter and voices, clinking of cutlery, and dogs whining and barking receded into the distance. I wanted to lie down in the soft grass and pull him down on top of me, but he suddenly broke away.

"Not here, sweetheart. Not in public. Come with me to my hotel."

"Yes!" I nearly shouted, but he put his fingers on my mouth.

"Shh. Not so loud."

"Sorry," I whispered. "Where's your car?"

"I didn't drive here. I took a taxi. What about you?"

I tried to remember. "I…I…my God, I can't drive. I've been drinking. How stupid. I was going to stay here, with Jules tonight, but now…"

He laughed softly and pulled up the zip of my dress. "I think we'll have to put this on hold, my dear."

"On hold?" I stammered, feeling suddenly cold despite the warm breeze.

"Yeah," he grunted, smoothing his hair and pushing his shirt into his trousers. "This is not the time or the place. I don't know what came over me. You're just so delicious, and the champagne and the beautiful night and everything made me feel quite…amorous."

I stepped away, sobering up in an instant. What had I

been thinking? Snogging with my boss like a teenager. How unprofessional. How utterly stupid. I looked around to see if anyone had noticed us. Nobody was looking in our direction. Except Jonathan. Our eyes met across the expanse of lawn. He was too far away, and it was too dark to see his expression, but I could still sense his disappointment. My heart sank.

"Let's join the party," Kit said and took my hand.

I eased out of his grip. "No. I think I'll wait here for a bit. See you later."

"I'll be in touch." His lips grazed my cheek, and then he walked away, leaving me looking at the moon, wishing I could turn the clock back and undo what had just happened.

CHAPTER 11

We were busy the next few days, which helped me turn my mind away from the clinch with Kit. He tried to call me and left messages on my voicemail, but I didn't return them. I sent him a brief text message, saying I'd call him back "soon." The calls stopped and were replaced by very suggestive text messages on WhatsApp, including a selfie of him naked, wet from the shower, with the caption "look what you get if you practise." It made me giggle, but I didn't reply. I didn't know how to respond but had to admit to myself he looked pretty good from every angle.

I buried myself in work, getting stuck into the weight loss feature and the historical scandals articles. Dan took a few candid shots for my editor column, and I asked Jonathan to dig up some good stories for the "Fifty Shades of History" piece.

We announced the coming features in the online edition of the paper, and Dan got bold and said we should have a weekly weigh-in at the gym every Friday. He had got a few of the lads from the rugby club to join in, and Fidelma and Sinead managed to dragoon two of their friends to take part. "They've been yo-yo dieting for years," Fidelma said. "Now they can get serious about losing weight."

Joe, the personal trainer at the gym, had no objections to leading the project. It would help his business, he declared.

To my utter surprise, Pandora called me one evening and offered to help. "I'd like to launch the campaign at our new gym," she said. "And then we could do a raffle for a free day at the spa. Facial, massage, pool, free lunch. How's that?"

"Gosh, that's very generous," I replied.

"I think it'll be great for publicity," she said. "And fun. All I ever see are the guests and they're sooo boring. I'd love to join and help out with the campaign. I'd like to meet real people instead of these rich dudes who're only interested in golf and food. And the women? Never seen a duller bunch. Can't talk about anything except eyebrows and nails and clothes. Please let me help out. I could be campaign manager or something."

I couldn't believe I was hearing this. Pandora, the trophy wife wanted to help us out? "Don't you have to ask Richard for permission before you hand out free days at the spa?"

Pandora let out a throaty laugh. "Richard? Nah, I run this show. And it's mostly my dad's money that went into this hotel. He hasn't much of a say in the running of it. I married him for his looks, not his brain."

I smirked. So, Richard was the trophy husband, not the other way around, despite all his posturing and pretending to be the boss. "That'd be brilliant. Thank you, Pandora."

"You're welcome. But all of this is on one condition—that the whole campaign is focused on health, not on being super skinny."

I considered this for a moment and realised she was right. It had to be more about health, not looks. "Yes," I said after a while. "You're so right. That's exactly what it should be about. Can I hand it all over to you? And then you and the girls can work together."

"Fabulous," Pandora exclaimed. "This'll be such a blast."

"It'll take the pressure off me too. We'll work out the details later."

"Wonderful. This'll be so much fun. I can get Richard to take over in reception."

I hung up, still smiling. Wait till Dessie heard about it. She wasn't overly fond of Richard after all the misery he'd put her through when she was young. Now, here he was as Pandora's lapdog. *The mills of God grind slowly*, I thought. I had always believed that everyone eventually got their just deserts, now I felt Richard was getting his. And Dessie had finally found the happiness she deserved. Maybe I would also one day find mine? I felt sure it would happen. Ever the optimist, that's me.

* * *

Later that evening, Jonathan invited me to his place to look through some material he had come across. He also said we had to work out a deal about his involvement in the magazine. I sighed. I couldn't afford to pay him. But I had an idea he might like.

"How about a bit of bartering?" I asked as I joined him on the Chesterfield couch in his living room.

"Bartering?"

"Yeah. You know, offering something instead of money for a job."

"What's the something you have to offer?"

I pushed away the cheeky response I would have given in normal circumstances. "You need an editor for the book you're working on, don't you?"

"Yes, but…?"

I pointed at my chest. "Here she is! I'm an editor, you know. And I'll edit your book in exchange for your work on the historical series."

He looked at me for a moment. "That sounds like a very good exchange of services. I would normally pay more than five hundred euros for an edit of a forty-thousand-word book. It would be a full copy edit, two passes and proofreading?"

I nodded. "That's right. And in exchange you would write a weekly piece about an historical saucy scandal. Does that seem fair to you?"

"Not usually, no. But for this magazine? Absolutely."

"Deal." I pretended to spit into my hand before I held it out.

Jonathan laughed and shook my hand so hard I squealed. "Oops. Sorry."

I shook my hand in the air. "You have a very firm grip for a—" I stopped abruptly. I was going to say "gay guy" but realised in time what a faux pas that would be.

"A what?"

"A historian," I said, trying to cover up my mistake. "I mean, you don't look the bodybuilder type or anything."

He shrugged. "No, I'm more of a nerd, really. Unlike your boss, who's kind of bulky in all the right places, no?"

"No. No, no, no!" I put my hands over my face. "Listen, about what happened at the party. I know you saw me with Kit. It was a mistake. I was a little tipsy and got carried away. I've been kicking myself ever since, wishing it hadn't happened." I sighed and looked at him. "Oh God, how I wish that hadn't happened. It was so *utterly* stupid. I don't even like the guy."

"But he turns you on? Isn't that what you said?" The concern in his eyes touched my heart in a strange way.

"Yes," I replied. "That's my problem with that man. I don't like him, and I doubt he likes me very much, but we're so drawn to each other physically. It's something I can't control. I don't know what to do. What would you do?"

"Me?" He looked alarmed. "Can't say I've ever been in that situation. I've been in love, of course. And my heart has been broken twice in my life. It hurts a lot. The last time, I was totally pinned to the wall for over a year. But my work and doing the dig and writing this book helped. It's good to get so involved in a project that you love. All-absorbing and healing."

I took his hand. "I'm sorry. I know how hard that is. I'm still trying to get over someone. Nearly there, but I don't think the scars will ever be gone. Strange. We were only involved a couple of weeks, but…"

"And now you have the hots for that other guy? Love and lust. Sometimes they don't come together."

"That's true." Our eyes met. I suddenly knew that here was a person I could truly love—whom I loved already despite only knowing him for a few weeks. But it was a spiritual love, not a physical one. The look in his eyes mirrored my thoughts. He felt the same for me. It wasn't about sex and probably never would be, but our spirits seemed to meet and entwine that moment as the warm summer wind blew in through the open window, and a lone blackbird sang in the garden below.

Jonathan slowly withdrew his hand. "I can't tell you what to do. I should say 'Don't get involved,' but that is something you have to decide for yourself."

"I know. I'm a grown-up. I'll handle it." I looked at the papers on the coffee table. "Okay, so let's get stuck in. What have you got here?"

"A few sad stories. I think we should start with this one." He pulled out a piece of paper. "This is a story of a monk and a nun whose love letters were found in the old garden of the little abbey outside town."

"But there's only one wall and an arch left."

"That's right. But they did an archaeological dig there and found all kinds of things. The letters were in a silver box, which saved them from deteriorating."

"Okay. Go on. What's the story?"

"Around the middle of the twelfth century, Father Peter O'Malley came to the abbey to work on the books the monks were making there. Prayer books, I think. You know, the ones with those beautiful illustrations. They're in Trinity College along with the *Book of Kells*. Anyway, while he was there, he came into contact with a young nun, Sister Anna. I think the nuns used to serve food to the monks or something. In any case, they fell in love and even had a child."

"Wow," I gasped. "How did they manage that?"

"There was a secret tunnel between the convent and the monastery. Built as an escape route in case the Vikings attacked. They used it to meet up somewhere."

"So what happened?"

"We don't really know. All we have are these letters. They're quite steamy even by today's standards. We also have an old portrait of Sister Anna, painted before she joined the convent." He pulled out a photocopy.

I peered at the portrait of a young woman in a medieval headdress. "She's very beautiful. Just look at those eyes."

"I'd say she drove Father Peter mad with desire."

"Can we print the letters? Or parts of them anyway?"

"The originals are in Latin. But a friend of mine who's a Latin scholar translated some of them a few years ago. I'll get in touch with her and see if she'd agree to let me publish them—or parts of them anyway."

"We'd only need the story and a bit of a letter—a saucy bit, if that's possible."

He winked at me. "Definitely. And I'll e-mail you a better copy of the portrait. That's also in the Trinity archives."

I got up. "Good. So that's all settled then. Must get back to finishing the online issue that'll go live later this week. We'll announce the weight loss feature and the history one too. Then I have to—God help me—speak to Kit and clear all this with him before we start writing it up."

Jonathan punched me playfully on the shoulder. "Stay strong. Don't give in. And don't listen to his sweet talking."

"I'll do my best." I blew him a kiss and walked down the stairs, feeling our friendship had taken quite a different turn.

* * *

Even though my talk with Jonathan had strengthened my resolve to resist Kit, his low, sexy voice on the phone later that night made me tingle in all the wrong places. Maybe it was the warm night, the two glasses of wine I had drunk, or the fact that I was in bed wearing only the flimsiest of nightgowns, but our conversation veered off into forbidden territory—forbidden for me, but not him.

"Are you in bed?" he started. "You sound a little sleepy, so you must be. Wish I was there with you."

"Were," I mumbled, stretching out my legs under the sheet.

"What?"

"It has to be 'wish I were.' Sorry, I'm a bit of a grammar police. Comes with the territory."

"What territory? Being a bluestocking?"

"No, being an editor. It's too hot for stockings."

"Oh yes, I know," he purred. "But I love the image of you in stockings. I can imagine sliding my hand over the top and feeling the silky skin of your—"

I sat up. "Kit, I didn't call you to have phone sex. This was meant to be a professional call."

"What profession would that be, then?" he inquired, his silky voice brimming with laughter.

"Shut up and listen," I snapped.

"Yes, my little dominatrix. Are you going to whip me? In that case, should I be naked?"

I closed my eyes for a second, pushing away the image of a naked Kit. "No. Please try to concentrate on what I'm saying, okay?"

"Okay, sweet girl. Go ahead. I'm all ears."

"Well, first of all, we have a few additional ideas for the magazine, but that doesn't really—or shouldn't—concern you. I have the powers to make all the executive decisions for the newspaper and the magazine, right?"

"Of course, my dear."

"Then," I breezed on, "there's just the matter of distribution. I sent a copy of the magazine to Keatings. They're the biggest—or I should say the only—bookstore chain in Ireland. They're also the main sellers of magazines and newspapers here. You don't own them, do you?"

"Keatings? No, not as far as I know."

"Thought not." I lay back against the pillows again. "I'm hoping they'll want to distribute the magazine to all their bookstores in Ireland. If they do, we could be looking at a huge boost in circulation. Just an idea I have. They'll probably say no, but you have to try everything."

"How many stores do they have?"

"More than sixty. They're also in Northern Ireland, which makes them a UK chain too," I babbled on, eager to keep the conversation cool.

"Sounds good. How does this involve me?"

"I think it could mean signing some kind of contract. If they agree, that is."

"I see," he muttered. "Well, if they agree to distribute, tell them to get in touch with my lawyers. I'll send you their contact details."

"Okay, I will." I paused. "So that's it then."

"Not quite." He was purring again. "I have something to ask you."

I sighed. "Please, Kit. I thought I made it clear I'm not going to—"

"I'm leaving," he interrupted. "Going back to London."

"Oh. Okay," I said, keeping my voice neutral. "Have a great trip back."

"Not so fast. I'm not going until the day after tomorrow. How about dinner here at the hotel tomorrow evening? If you dare, that is," he added.

"Of course I do. What time?"

"Eight o'clock?"

"I'll be there."

"Looking forward to seeing you. Wear something—"

I hung up before he had a chance to finish. I curled up in a ball under the sheet. *Oh God, what have I done? Agreed to have dinner at his hotel. How very unwise.* But I had done it to prove to myself that I could resist him. If I didn't, I'd lose my self-respect forever. *Why does it have to be like this? Feeling physically drawn to a man I don't like very much and loving a man platonically, who would never— Or would he?* I stopped my thoughts right there. I had to clear this up once and for all. It was late, but it couldn't wait. I had to know.

I got out of bed, flung on the linen shirt I used as a dressing gown in the summer, and marched across the flat, through the front door, and rang Liz's doorbell, long and hard.

A few moments later, the door opened, and Liz, in pink pyjamas, a sleep mask on top of her head, peered sleepily at me. "What's going on? Is there a fire?"

"No. Sorry to wake you. But I have a very important question to ask you."

Liz blinked. "What did you say?"

"I have a very—"

"Hang on." Liz dug in her ear and removed something that seemed to be stuck there. "Earplugs. I wear them because of the dawn chorus at four in the morning. Go on."

"Okay." I cleared my throat. "I have to ask you—" I lowered my voice "—is Jonathan really...Is he...gay?" I whispered.

CHAPTER 12

Liz stared at me and blinked twice. "What?" She backed away from the door. "Come inside. He might hear us."

"Okay." I stepped inside and closed the door behind me. "So?"

"Come into the living room. I think we need to talk."

I followed her into her cosy living room as she switched on lights and opened the window to let in the cool night air. "It's a little stuffy in here. I haven't been here much in this hot weather. I usually sit in the garden in the evenings."

"This is a nice space, though," I said, looking at the comfortable chairs, the sofa covered in a patchwork quilt, and the bookcase crammed with paperbacks. One corner was taken up with her yoga equipment—mat and foam blocks—shared with a small bronze Buddha, and lavender-scented candles, which, even unlit, spread their soothing scent through the room.

"Sit down, and I'll make us some camomile tea," Liz said.

"Thank you." I sat down in the sofa and immediately felt a strange peace come over me. I didn't know if it was the scent of lavender, the sound of Liz making tea in the kitchen, or the soft breeze blowing through the open window, but suddenly, all my worries seemed insignificant.

Liz carried in a tray with two mugs and a plate of oatmeal biscuits and put them on the coffee table. She handed me a mug and joined me on the sofa. "Here. This'll help you calm down."

"Thank you." I took the mug and breathed in the scent of camomile. "I'm already calm. This room is so soothing. And you have a very restful aura."

She smiled. "Comes with age, I suppose. And you know what? The older I get, the younger I feel. I mean, I get more and more childlike. I no longer notice people's race, colour, religion, or age. I see their spirits more and more clearly."

"That sounds wonderful. Very inspirational."

Liz shrugged. "I'm perhaps more philosophical, that's all. But about Jonathan…?"

I sat up, spilling camomile tea on my chest. "Yes?"

"Why do you ask? Is this important to you all of a sudden?"

"Yes," I said hotly. "It is. I need to know because… because—"

"Never mind. No need to explain. But the answer to your question is—no. Jonathan is not gay. I've known him for over two years, right through his engagement with that woman in Dublin and after the breakup, so I can say this with absolute certainty. Why did you think he was?"

My heart skipped a beat. "He isn't? But I thought…when you said that he's very close to his feminine side—"

"—that it was another way of saying he's gay?"

I nodded. "Yes. I assumed you were being discreet but still giving me the message."

"God, no," Liz exclaimed. "I would never do that. People's sexual preferences are their own business. I just meant what I said, that Jonathan is close to his feminine side. It's one of his many wonderful qualities. Don't you think?"

"Definitely." I shook my head and laughed. "How stupid of me. And all this time I've been pouring my heart out to him about my problems with men and all my other woes, thinking he was my best friend."

Liz looked puzzled. "Why wouldn't he be? I mean, can't you have a friend who's male and straight?"

"Yes, I suppose. But a gay guy is like a girlfriend, only better. He's a man, but there's no sexual tension. But then if he's straight, it makes you think of him differently. How horrible that I've been blabbing about my own problems and never listened to his. A broken engagement, Jules said. That must have been so hard." I stared into the tea, not wanting to meet Liz's eyes. "Apart from him listening to my miseries, there is this connection…this love between us. We're kindred spirits, really. It felt like a perfect, platonic relationship, a meeting of minds, of thoughts and feelings, nothing physical. I felt safe with him."

"Why can't you still feel safe?"

I stared at Liz. "I don't know. Maybe because he might be attracted to me? Or me to him? Not that he's been flirty or anything."

"I'd say he's one of those slow burners. He probably wants to enjoy your friendship first and wait before anything else develops. And he's right. We all want things to happen so fast these days. Isn't it better to wait, to hold on and enjoy the friendship?" Liz leaned forward and put her hand on my cheek. "Stop being so frantic, Audrey. Relax and go with the flow. Enjoy what you have now, because now is all we have. Who knows what's in the future?" She leaned back and looked at me with those wise, calm eyes.

I let out a long sigh. "You're so right, Liz. Why didn't I come to you before?"

She laughed and picked up her mug, taking a sip. "I'm no guru or saint. I've been avoiding you lately, actually."

"You have? Why?"

She put her mug on the tray. "Oh, well, maybe it's too soon to say this, but Sean and I have been seeing each other quite a bit during the past weeks. I didn't know where it was going, or how you'd feel about it, so I thought I'd wait. But now, tonight, I feel we should lay all our cards on the table, so to speak."

My mind was spinning. "Sean? You mean my father? You and Dad have been—"

Liz let out a girlish giggle. "No, we haven't gone all the way. But that might happen soon, I feel."

I cringed. "Uh, okay." I tried to push away the image of Dad and Liz in bed.

She laughed. "I can see that makes you uncomfortable. But hey, give us a break. We might be old, but we're not dead yet. I'm only sixty-three, your dad's sixty-five. Not exactly ancient. We still have those feelings, those urges and needs, and if it works, it's fabulous."

I looked at the floor, fighting an urge to stand up and scream, "TMI!" But what right did I have? Shouldn't I be happy for Dad? So they'd end up having sex—why shouldn't they? *Grow up, Audrey*, I said to myself. Liz was a very attractive woman. The laughter lines around her eyes and the few wrinkles around her mouth emphasised her fine features. Her body was strong and lithe, and she seemed both self-contained and serene. Added to that was her sense of humour and intelligence. I realised she and Dad would be perfect for each other, if it weren't for— "What about his sorrow?" I asked. "He still grieves for my mother."

Liz nodded. "Yes, I know. And he always will. I have to accept that. We talk about it, about *her* sometimes. I know, to use an old cliché, that there will probably always be three people in this relationship, but that's fine with me. Someone who is capable of such undying love must be admired, not criticised." She shook her head. "Oh, it's a little complicated. But we'll work it out. I know I said take it slowly just now, but at our age we don't have as much time." She looked at me with a touch of nervousness. "You don't mind? About us? If it were to become more serious?"

"Of course not." I moved closer and put my arms around her. "I think it's pretty perfect."

She patted my cheek. "Good. I'm happy. I'll never be your mother, but I'll always be your friend."

I sat back and smiled. "I couldn't wish for anything better." I yawned. "I'd better get some sleep and leave you to go back to bed. I have a heavy day tomorrow, followed by a heavy evening."

"Heavy evening?"

I sighed. "Yes. I've agreed to have dinner with my rather sexy but not so loveable boss. He keeps trying to get me into bed." I looked at Liz. "One day he'll succeed. I can feel it."

She rolled her eyes. "One of those, huh? I've come across one or two in my not-so-pure youth. The sexy but unlovable ones are hell to resist if you have a penchant for bad boys."

I laughed despite my anguish. "You too?"

She sighed. "Oh yes. I slept with a few of them, and it never brought me anything but misery. Before I met my husband, of course. I was a career woman with an important job in a pharmaceutical company. I came across a lot of men I should have stayed away from. But it was like an itch I had to scratch, if you see what I mean."

I could imagine her as young and sexy and—very like me. "So what should I do?" I asked.

She leaned forward and looked into my eyes. "Don't scratch that itch."

CHAPTER 13

Despite my resolve to follow Liz's advice, I made an effort to look good for my dinner with Kit. Not too sexy or glamorous, just good. *Good enough to eat*, I thought as I did a twirl in front of the mirror in my bedroom. I had found a navy silk dress I'd bought for a press dinner in Dublin the year before.

With my hair up, a gold cuff on my wrist the only jewellery, and just a touch of make-up, I felt I had struck the right note—fashionable career woman dining with her boss. Simple, classy, and just a tad sexy. I blew myself a kiss, grabbed my purse, and set off for Killybeg Hotel and Spa. I was a little early, but I had arranged to meet Pandora to discuss our weight loss feature. She said she had some ideas to make it spectacular.

Ten minutes later, I pulled up in front of the steps, handed the car keys to the valet, and ran into reception, where I found Richard doing the job as receptionist in a blue suit with a brass pin in his lapel that said "Manager."

"Hi, Richard," I said, "You look cute."

His face reddened. "What can I do for you?"

"I'm looking for Pandora."

"She said she'd see you in the library," Richard replied curtly. "She's on the phone to her dad in New York, so she'll be a little late."

"The library?" I asked.

"Yes." He pointed down the long gallery. "It's on the left, beside the dining room."

I thanked him, walked down the gallery into the library, and was instantly enchanted. This room had not been stripped of its books or contents before the big auction the year before and had been slowly and painstakingly restored to exactly what it would have been like in the early 1800s. The oak panelling and the bookcases had been polished, the oriental carpet cleaned, and the missing books in the collection replenished with identical leather-bound replicas. The muted colours of the carpet and the spines of the books glowed in the soft light, and the room smelled of woodsmoke and old leather. It was the most beautiful room I had even been in.

I padded across the carpet and peered at the books, pulling out *Sense and Sensibility* just to see which edition it was. The flyleaf said 1887. I sat down in one of the green velvet sofas, flicked the pages, and started to read, amazed at how the words of Jane Austen could still draw me into the story.

I was deeply absorbed in the fate of the Dashwood family when someone tapped me on the shoulder.

It was Pandora. "Hi, Audrey. Enjoying the library?"

"Loving it. I could move in here and read from start to finish. You've done a wonderful job."

"Thank you. I got an interior designer from London to do it." She looked at the book. "What's that you're reading?"

"Jane Austen. *Sense and Sensibility*. Have you read it?"

"No. I'm not much of a reader." Pandora plonked herself down beside me. "But I saw that old version of *Pride and Prejudice* recently. Colin Firth in the wet shirt was the best thing in it."

I closed the book. "Not quite my take on that story, but I know what you mean. Anyway, about the feature? I have a dinner appointment in about twenty minutes, so we'd better get started."

She winked. "I know. With Kit. He booked a quiet table."

"It's a working dinner," I said primly.

She smirked. "Yeah, right. You look really professional in that killer dress."

I pulled the skirt over my knees. "Thank you."

"I'm only teasing you. He booked a table for three, so it must be about work, then."

I blinked. "Three? He didn't tell me he was inviting someone else."

"Well, whatever. You'll find out soon enough." Pandora pulled some papers from the folder she was holding. "I've made up a few main points for our feature."

"Thanks." I looked at the notes. "No diets?"

"I don't believe in diets." Her eyes were suddenly full of pain. "I've been there, you know. Anorexia, bulimia, the lot. I know how you can be totally screwed up by body image and dieting."

"You do?" I glanced at her full figure.

"You wouldn't know," she said hotly. "You didn't grow up on Park Avenue."

"No. But I have a feeling—"

"Screw your feelings," Pandora said harshly. "If we're going to do this, let's do it right. It shouldn't be about diets and body image, it should be about what makes you feel good. And if you feel good, you look good, even if you're not a size zero."

"Of course." I nodded as I read the notes. "I see what you mean. I like this. Not many changes in diet, just cutting down and trying to eat more fruit and veg. Plus exercise every day in some form. It's simple really, and keeping it simple is the best way."

"Simple but hard for so many. Not that you'd know, of course."

"You're right, I wouldn't. I've never had problems with weight. Must be my metabolism or something."

"You probably don't reach for chocolate or pizza when you're down."

"No. My comfort is reading. I love escaping into a story when things get rough. That's what I've always done, ever since my mother died. I think she must have taught me that." I shrugged. "I don't remember. I was only seven."

Pandora put her hand on mine. "Oh, Audrey, I'm so sorry. I had no idea. How hard that must have been."

I patted her hand. "Thanks. Yes, it was, but I had a great dad. We went through a lot together, but we had each other." I glanced at the old carriage clock on the mantelpiece. "I'd better go. It's eight o'clock. Kit and his guest will be expecting me."

Pandora gathered up her notes. "Okay. We're nearly done anyway."

I got up. "Could you get in touch with Mary so she can write all this up? You could come into the office to work out the plan with the editorial team. Tomorrow, perhaps?"

Pandora brightened. "That would be awesome! Thank you, Audrey. I'll do all I can to help get this feature off the ground."

"Brilliant. Thanks, Pandora. I'll talk to you tomorrow. I'd better get into the dining room now."

She blew me a kiss. "Have a great evening. And—be careful."

"I'll do my best."

* * *

Butterflies whirled in my stomach as I made my way to the elegant dining room, where a waiter showed me to a table laid for three at the back of the room. "Mr Montgomery will be here shortly," he said as he pulled out my chair. "He's gone to the entrance hall to receive his guest."

"That's fine. Thank you." I sat down, jumping as the waiter snapped a linen napkin the size of a kitchen towel onto my lap. I smiled at him as he lit the candles. I wasn't used to five-star restaurants. But Kit walking into the dining room, a gorgeous black man in tow, made me forget my discomfort. Both dressed in dark trousers and white shirts open at the neck, they couldn't be more different. I couldn't take my eyes off the stranger. He looked like a clone of a young Harry Belafonte. I nearly expected him to burst into some calypso melody at any moment. I watched as he walked with catlike grace behind Kit, his slim hips swivelling slightly as they rounded the last table. They came to a stop in front of me.

"Evening, Audrey," Kit said and kissed me on the cheek. "May I introduce Geoff Thornton, my managing director?"

I held out my hand to the Harry Belafonte lookalike. "Hello, nice to meet you."

His smile lit up the whole room as his warm hand gripped mine. "Hello, Audrey. The pleasure is entirely mine, I can assure you." His strong Scottish accent surprised me. I had been expecting something more Trinidadian.

Kit laughed and pulled out a chair. "Geoff, please sit down and behave yourself. This is a business meeting."

Still grinning, Geoff sat down. "I know. But a very pleasant one, I have to say. Don't you think, Audrey?"

I smiled back at him. "Absolutely."

"Right," Kit grunted and opened the menu the waiter handed him. "We'll order and get to business. Let's not faff around with starters, okay? I know the beef is excellent here, so how about filet mignon with duchess potatoes?"

"Okay," Geoff and I said in unison as we looked into each other's eyes.

"A glass of Bordeaux each and a side order of salad," Kit said to the waiter. "Beef medium rare all around?"

"Rare for me," I said, tearing myself away from Geoff's velvet eyes.

"Same here," he said.

Kit flicked the menu back to the waiter. "That's it, then. We'll let you know about anything else later."

"Very well, sir." The waiter topped up our water glasses and disappeared.

Kit wiped his brow and glanced out the window. "Very hot today, isn't it? And those dark clouds rolling in must mean there's a thunderstorm on the way."

I took a sip of water. "Yes, that's what the weather forecast said. Then more heat tomorrow. This has been an amazing summer." I looked at Geoff. "Is this your first visit to Ireland?"

He nodded. "Yes, but not my last. This is such a beautiful country. Very like Scotland in some ways."

"I've never been to Scotland," I said. "I'd love to see it someday."

Geoff smiled. "If you do go, please let me know."

"I will."

"Yes, fine," Kit interrupted. "But let's get down to business. I asked Geoff to come here so he could explain the details of a very exciting offer we want to make you."

Confused, I stared at him. "Offer? What kind of offer? I know you hinted at something like that a while back, but I thought you were having me on.... Aren't we here to discuss the magazine?"

"The magazine? Great work, I have to say," Geoff stated. "Really good country publication."

"Yes. Very good effort," Kit cut in. "I finally had a chance to take a look at it. Very nice."

"Thanks for the faint praise," I snipped. "But what's this meeting all about then, if it's not about that?"

We were interrupted by two waiters bringing us our order. We were silent while they fussed with plates, wine, salad, and bread. Then Kit picked up his wine glass.

"A toast," he said. "To our continued collaboration." He exchanged an odd look of complicity with Geoff and nodded.

As if on cue, Geoff took his glass and held it up, smiling at me. "To a lovely woman who lights up this dark evening with her beauty. Looking forward to working with you."

I lifted my glass with a feeling of dread. What were they up to? "Okay, thanks. Cheers," was all I managed. Then I said, "Working with me? What do you mean?"

They looked at each other again. Kit cleared his throat. "Have you heard of *The Bluestocking Review?*"

I laughed. "Heard of it? It's only the best literary magazine in Europe. I've subscribed to it for years. Love it."

Kit smiled. "Thought so. The good news is that we've just bought it."

I stared at him. "Really? How exciting. Great move, Kit. Congratulations."

"Thank you. It wasn't cheap. But the bad news is that the editor-in-chief, Majella Kastrup, is retiring in August."

"Oh nooo," I moaned. "That's terrible. I love her reviews. She's one of the best reviewers around."

Geoff sighed. "Absolutely. But—" he glanced at Kit "—that's what we wanted to talk to you about. You see," he continued, "we think you'd be perfect for her job."

I gasped. "What? Her job? You mean—"

Kit took my hand. "Yes, darling girl. We want you to take over as editor-in-chief of *The Bluestocking Review*. That's the offer we were talking about."

My head was spinning. Editor-in-chief of *The Bluestocking Review*? Me? Was I dreaming? I felt like pinching myself. An offer every journalist would dream of. It would mean— "What exactly will this mean?" I asked out loud. "I mean, wow, it's like, I don't know, landing a Hollywood film deal or something. But maybe I'm dreaming? Please pinch me so I can wake up."

Kit winked. "Where do you want me to pinch you? You're not dreaming, but I don't mind pinching you anyway."

"But…but," I stammered. "I'm not sure I'm qualified. What makes you think I am?"

"You have a degree in journalism," Geoff replied, "and I also believe you have a PhD in English literature from Trinity College?"

"Yes, but that doesn't mean—"

Kit took my hand. "Audrey, you have, in no time at all, turned the failing newspaper here around and also produced a very good magazine. All with just a few people to help you. This speaks volumes about your entrepreneurship and talent as an editor. You'd be perfect for *The Bluestocking Review*."

"Gosh," I said. "Yeah, but—" But what about the paper, I wanted to ask. *The Knockmealdown News* was very important to me. So were the people working with me to produce it every week. And the magazine? And, oh God, my flat and my new friends. My whole life here in this little town that I loved would be coming to an end. "And my cat," I said out loud.

"Cat?" Kit stared at me as he was cutting into his steak. "You have a cat? But can't you bring it to London? Cats live happily in flats in London, you know."

"Maybe," I said without conviction.

Geoff picked up his knife and fork. "I know it must have come as a shock, but let's not waste this delicious meal. Let it sink in, Audrey, and then we'll talk."

I poked at the food while they ate, still trying to get my head around what they had just said. I tried to imagine what it would be like to live in London and be the editor of this high-profile literary magazine. I knew it was run by a big staff of very talented women. My whole life seemed suddenly to have been turned upside down. Dad would be over the moon. This is what he'd wanted for me ever since I started college. But how would it feel to leave *The Knockmealdown News* to someone else?

"I won't be able to leave straight away," I said out loud. "I mean we're still trying to get our circulation up to what it was before the fire. If not, you're going to close it down, right?"

Kit nodded. "I'm afraid so. I'm sorry, sweetheart, it doesn't look good at the moment."

I stared at him. "What do you mean? I told you about Keatings. There's a good chance they'll want to distribute the magazine. And then we're away."

Kit shook his head with a glum expression. "I meant to tell you, but it got lost in the other stuff. I just heard from them. Unfortunately, they won't accept the kind of deal we were offering. They want a bigger discount."

My jaw dropped. "What? But that's impossible! We can't offer them more than 50 percent, otherwise we'd be selling at a loss. Shit. I was counting on them. I can't believe they would be so greedy."

Kit shrugged. "Yeah, well, that's business for you. Sorry about that. They said they liked the new magazine and wished you the best of luck."

"Fabulous," I muttered and attacked the steak with my knife. I cut off a big chunk and pushed it into my mouth. Even in all my nervousness, I had to admit it was delicious. Suddenly ravenous, I finished what was on my plate while the men continued to talk about *The Bluestocking Review* and certain changes they would like to make. It all sounded exciting, but my mind was still on *The Knockmealdown News* and what would happen to it.

"We must make sure we get good spots on national TV," Geoff said. "I'm sure Audrey would be fantastic on TV."

"Oh yes," Kit agreed. "That's partly why I wanted to offer her the job."

"Excuse me," I interrupted. "But when do you need to know if I'll accept the offer? Is there a deadline?"

Kit was about to reply but was interrupted by rumbling

outside that ended in a loud bang. The curtains billowed in a sudden gust of wind accompanied by the sound of torrential rain. "Holy shit," he exclaimed as the waiters ran to close the windows and the lights flickered. "That's some thunderstorm."

"We need the rain, though," I said. "But to come back to my question—when do you want my answer?"

There was a curious look in Kit's eyes. "I thought you might give us your answer right now."

I shook my head. "I need a little time. It's a big step. And I need to get someone to take over for me at the newspaper here."

Kit patted my hand and winked at Geoff. "Don't worry about that. We'll take care of everything."

I looked at him and wondered why his words sent a cold tingle down my spine.

CHAPTER 14

The following day, after a night with practically no sleep, I met with the staff to plan the launch of the weight loss feature we had decided to call "Fit for Life." I had e-mailed Pandora's notes to Mary, and she had turned them into a terrific article with bullet points for the diet and exercise recommendations. We also had Joe from the gym on board and a dietician friend of mine who had promised to write up a fact sheet. It was going to be terrific.

Pandora arrived at the office full of enthusiasm, and we soon got stuck into the plans for the launch and subsequent weigh-ins at the Killybeg gym. Everyone gathered around her, even Dan, who had started a diet and exercise routine with Joe. He was looking trimmer already, but that was probably because he pulled in his stomach and straightened his back as soon as Pandora sashayed into the office.

I felt a pang of sadness as I looked at my staff working with Pandora. What a wonderful team they were. I knew they all worked hard to make a decent living, even if it was a struggle for some of them. Mary was a single mother with two children, Fidelma was supporting her elderly parents, and Sinead was saving up to buy a house and finally move out of her parents' home. Dan had no real financial problems, but he had just told me the other day that he and Sally were getting serious and were planning to get engaged. What would happen to them when I left? What would happen to me? What a huge wrench it would be to leave them behind and move to an enormous city. I knew I could do the job I had just been offered, but the stress levels would be multiplied by several thousand.

But then I suddenly felt a spark of excitement when I thought of the night before and that job offer. Unbelievable. Me? The editor of the largest literary magazine in the UK? It didn't seem real. I hadn't told anyone yet. Maybe if I did, it would become more of a reality.

* * *

"I can't believe it really happened," I said to Jonathan later that day over tea in my garden, which was cool and fresh after the storm the night before.

"But it did, and you're ecstatic," he said, smiling at me over his mug.

"And scared." I gathered Cat into my lap and stroked her absent-mindedly. "It's so big and such a huge step. And I have just moved here and got to know you and Liz and started to put down roots." I looked at him, willing him to tell me what to do. "But I was thinking… I could commute. I could keep the flat and come here every weekend. There are flights to London from Cork several times a day. It wouldn't be that hard. Would it?"

Jonathan put his mug on the little garden table. "Are you telling me or asking me?"

"I suppose I'm asking you."

"In that case, the answer is: No, you can't."

"What do you mean?" I asked, taken aback by the hard edge in his voice.

He got up. "You can't have your cake and eat it, Audrey. You can't live in two places."

"Does this mean you think I should stay and not take the job?"

"I didn't say that. I can't make up your mind for you. You've been handed a fantastic offer of a job many would kill for. Your whole life will change. It's the biggest break you'll ever get. It won't come around again. But you have to delve into your own soul and ask yourself if you have what it takes. If you can live on the edge and cope with the stress of such a job."

"The job itself seems perfect," I mused.

"Maybe." Jonathan looked doubtful. "It won't all be about reading great books and writing reviews, you know. There will be a lot of tough decisions, and some of them will force you to act against your conscience. You're a beautiful, intelligent woman with only one slight handicap—your kindness and empathy for others. It'll be glamorous and exciting, of course, and you'll be in the limelight a lot of the time. But you might have to be ruthless and upset people with harsh reviews. Can you handle that?"

I looked up at him towering above me in my deckchair. "Yes. I think I can."

"Then that's okay. Go for it." He leaned down, put his hands on the arms of the chair and kissed me lightly on the mouth. "Good luck, girl. I'll be upstairs if you need me."

The kiss lingered on my lips long after he had walked out of my garden.

* * *

The thought of leaving was harder than I had imagined. I asked Dad to come over for dinner so I could tell him my news. I wanted to see the delight in his face when he heard it, hoping it would help me get over the leaving blues. I decided not to invite Liz. This was a father-daughter moment that could not be shared.

He was inside only two minutes when I told him.

He stared at me. Then a slow smile lit up his face, and he threw his arms around me. "I don't know what to say. I'm so proud of you. So, so proud, my darlin'." He held me at arm's length and looked at me with tears in his eyes. "Finally. You've arrived. I knew it would happen one day." He pulled me back again and squeezed me in a bone-crushing hug. "You clever girl."

I had to laugh. "I can't breathe. Let me go." I struggled out of his embrace. "I knew you'd be pleased."

"Of course I am. But you? Are you happy? Excited? How do you feel?"

"Overwhelmed." I sat down in my mother's chair by the fireplace, while Dad perched on the arm of the sofa. "I'm scared. And sad about having to leave. I haven't told anyone yet except Jonathan. I haven't even formally accepted the position. I have another week before I have to say yes or no."

Dad stared at me. "No? There's no question of you not accepting, is there?"

"No, of course not. It's the chance of a lifetime. It'd be bonkers to say no. Not that I'm happy about leaving *The Knockmealdown News* and the wonderful people who work there, of course. How are they going to cope without me?"

"Nobody is irreplaceable," Dad said.

"I know. And this is a good time to leave. The magazine took off nicely and will keep the paper going. If we'd got the deal with Keatings and the countrywide distribution deal, I wouldn't have even contemplated leaving. Then we would have been facing quite a challenge, making it a bigger operation altogether." I sighed. "But we didn't. They couldn't accept the discount and wanted more, which we couldn't afford. Pity." I looked around the living room. "The biggest wrench will be leaving this flat. I love it. It feels like home."

Dad smiled. "Maybe you don't have to."

"What do you mean? I'm moving to London!"

"Just an idea. Something that occurred to me. I'll tell you in a minute." He got up. "Do I smell food? I'm quite hungry. Didn't you say something about dinner?"

I jumped up. "Oh my God, the casserole! I made you chicken with mushrooms. Your favourite."

Dad followed me into the kitchen, where I rescued the casserole that was simmering on the stove. I fished some only slightly singed garlic bread and two charred baked potatoes out of the oven and served the dinner. Minutes later, I looked at Dad across the kitchen table.

"So, come on, what was that about not having to leave this flat?"

He finished his mouthful. "You could sublet it. To me."

I put down my fork. "To you? What are you going to do with it?"

"Live here, of course." He coloured slightly, pretending to adjust the napkin in his lap. "You see, Liz and I—"

"I know." I smiled at him. "You're dating."

"You make me sound like a teenager. But okay, we're seeing each other. And we like each other. A lot." He looked at me with a touch of nervousness. "You don't mind?"

"Why should I mind? I think it's terrific. Liz is fab. Go for it, Dad."

He laughed. "Hold on, girl. For now it's a friendship that is rather lovely. No more."

"And no less," I quipped. "I get it now. You want to come and live here, just across the hall from Liz, but still keep your independence. Am I right?"

Dad smiled ruefully. "You have me taped as usual. But yes, that's what I'm thinking. It suddenly dawned on me when you were talking about moving and how sad you were to leave this flat. I'm selling the house when I retire, so this will be a perfect base while I look around for something to buy. I can keep my tools in the little greenhouse at the back if Jonathan agrees. I'm planning to set up a small business in this area, you see."

"Doing what?"

He grinned. "Fixing things. You know, like putting up shelves and painting walls and wallpapering and all those things most people find a pain in the neck. I'll even put together IKEA furniture. I'll be 'Handyman Sean.' What do you think?"

"Brilliant idea, Dad. You'll make millions."

"Well, not quite. But I could make a bit of extra money to top up my pension while having fun. Win-win for me. So, if you agree, I'll move in here and look after everything, including the cat. What do you say?"

I sighed, my heart lighter. "Dad, you're an angel. I love you. It's the perfect solution. Come on, let's finish dinner and then go and see if we can get a hold of Jonathan."

He nodded and dug into his chicken casserole again. "This is delicious."

"No, it's not. It's overcooked and stringy because I forgot about it. I'm sorry."

"It's not every day you get an offer of a job in London."

I looked at his dear face, and suddenly, my eyes filled with tears. "I'm going to miss you."

His smile was tinged with sadness. "Me too. But it's time to cut the umbilical. You're an adult now. You have to go out into the world and shine for your old dad."

I wiped my eyes with my napkin. "I know. I will. I'll make you proud. And in any case, if you take over my flat, I can come and visit whenever I want."

"Of course you can. But big cities have a habit of swallowing you up. You might get too busy to come over."

"I'll make time," I said without conviction, knowing what he said was true.

He got up and put his plate on the draining board. "Let's find Jonathan. We'll have to plead with him to let me have the flat."

"You go and plead. I'll tidy up here. Bring Jonathan down

for coffee and apple pie when you've finished talking."

"Okay." He smoothed his hair and straightened his shirt collar. "Do I look all right? Like the model tenant?"

I blew him a kiss. "You look perfect. Anyone would kill to have you."

He put up a thumb and left. I turned my attention to the dishes, wishing yet again things were different and I didn't have to take that big step. "I'm such a chicken," I said to Cat, who was slinking around my legs, meowing as if she hadn't been fed in days. "I wish I could stay here and run the paper and have a quiet life. But I can't, can I?"

Cat looked up at me, her tail swishing, and meowed loudly.

I put a piece of leftover chicken in her bowl. "You're right. I have to go and conquer London. And Kit." I suddenly froze. What had I just said? Kit? Was that why I was going to London? For him? I shook my head. "No, it's for me," I said out loud. "Isn't it?"

Cat didn't reply. Having finished the chicken, she sat in a pool of sunlight on the tiles, cleaning her face, looking at me as if she could see into my soul and didn't really like what she saw.

* * *

I tidied the kitchen, dried the dishes, and put everything away. I took the apple pie out of the fridge and put it in the oven for a few minutes while I whipped the cream. Twenty minutes later, the coffee table in the living room was set with plates, warm apple pie, and whipped cream, but there was still no sign of Dad or Jonathan. Where were they? I opened the door to the hall and listened. Nothing except a murmur of male voices from upstairs. Were they arguing? I tiptoed halfway up and stopped again to listen. No arguing, but laughter. Dad's voice saying, "This is great beer. Belgian?"

Jonathan replied something I couldn't hear.

Then Dad. "Another? Yes, please."

Bloody hell! They were drinking beer and having fun. Dad had completely forgotten me and my apple pie. Men! I stomped up the stairs and flung open the door to Jonathan's flat. "Hey, you," I snapped. "Enough of the male bonding. I have apple pie and coffee for you downstairs. You completely forgot about it, didn't you, Dad?"

Dad, sitting on a bar stool by the counter that divided the living room and the kitchen smiled sheepishly at me. "Yeah, well, we're celebrating. We've just negotiated the deal, and we thought we'd drink to it."

Jonathan stood behind the bar opening a bottle. He raised it and smiled at me. "Do you want a beer? It's Belgian. The best."

I sighed and took the bottle. "Okay. If you can't beat 'em, join 'em, right?" I took a slug, drank too fast and coughed. "Sorry. Yes. Great beer. What's the deal you've negotiated?"

"Your flat," Dad said. "Meet your new tenant."

"I hope you'll be happy together," I said. "It was Dad's idea, though."

Jonathan beamed at me over his beer. "Great idea. Couldn't have come up with a better one myself. I'm impressed. And we have also agreed that Sean will fix anything that's broken in the house. He'll even do plumbing."

"But not electricity," Dad cut in. "With plumbing you only risk getting wet. Electricity will kill you stone dead."

"We wouldn't want that," Jonathan quipped.

"And I can keep my tools in the greenhouse if I leave a little room for Jonathan's wine rack." Dad smiled at Jonathan.

I took another slug of beer. It really was delicious. "Everything falls into place. I bet you can't wait for me to move out now, right?"

"When are you moving?" Jonathan asked.

I sat down on the bar stool beside Dad's. "I'm not sure. I haven't even told them I'm taking the job. I also have to organise a successor here at the paper. But that won't be a problem. I'm going to suggest Dan. He's been with the paper for ten years, ever since he graduated from college. He knows the ropes, even if he tends to be a little unsure of himself."

"Maybe he'll feel better when you're not there breathing down his neck?" Jonathan suggested.

"What do you mean?" I snapped. "I don't breathe down his neck. Or anyone's neck."

Jonathan winked at Dad. "Of course not, Miss Control Freak. I've seen you in action. You have this nit-picking streak. Not your fault, but I'm sure it's a little nerve-racking."

"Jonathan's right," Dad cut in. "You're a bit of a perfectionist at times. Which is a good thing," he added hastily when I glared at him. "Makes everything you do perfect. What's wrong with that?"

"Absolutely nothing." Jonathan smirked. "I wish I were as perfect as Audrey."

"That perfection comes from insecurity," Dad said.

I frowned. "What do you mean?"

"I read something about that in an article."

Jonathan nodded. "I know. It's a way of making one feel safe. Trying to control the world so nothing bad can happen."

"Oh, puleese." I rolled my eyes and put the bottle on the counter. "I'll leave you to finish the psychoanalysis. I'm going for a walk. Don't forget the apple pie downstairs."

I walked down the stairs, longing for a breath of fresh air. It had been a hectic week with a lot of soul-searching and stress. I needed to be by myself for a bit. I went into my flat to change my shoes. That done, I walked out of the building into the street, where I could see the sun slowly setting behind the church tower. The air was soft, and the breeze cooled my hot cheeks. As I walked on, past houses and gardens full of flowers and rose bushes, through the park and further down the street to the path by the river, I suddenly felt I had to make it final. I stopped, hauled my phone out of my pocket, and punched in a number, waiting for a reply.

"Hello, Audrey." Kit's smoky voice made me smile.

"Yes, it's me. Hi. Sorry to call you so late, but I thought I'd let you know that I have decided to accept the offer." I started to walk while I waited for his response.

"Of course you have," Kit purred. "I knew you would, so I've set things in motion over here."

"Things? What things?"

"A press release is going out after the weekend, and we have arranged a TV interview with ITV and Sky News on Wednesday. I was just going to e-mail you the details and the dates so you could book your flight."

I suddenly felt dizzy. "Wow. That was quick."

"You need to be here on Sunday so you can prepare everything for the coming week. If you need a stylist, I can recommend a good one. You'll be meeting your new staff too, and you could perhaps also look around for living accommodation. I have looked up a few flats for rent in both Battersea and Chelsea you might go and see while you're here. Then you can fly back and sort things out at the office over there before your final move. We expect you to start on August 15th, which is a Monday."

"Oh." I stopped walking while my heartbeat increased alarmingly. "You've been busy."

"Things move fast in this business, sweetheart. Let me know when you've booked the flight."

"I will. I should tell you that I've decided to hand over my job here to Dan. He's the photographer but also—"

"Fine. Whatever. Talk soon. Bye," Kit muttered and hung up. He was obviously not interested in who took over *The Knockmealdown News*.

I walked to the bridge and leaned on the wall, looking

into the water. I could see trout dashing here and there, their scales glinting in the last few rays of the evening sun. But my mind wasn't on the fish. It was finally happening. I was moving to London. Jumbled thoughts whirled around in my head while my stomach churned. Sunday. I had to be there then. Only a couple of days away. So much happening over there. Meeting the new staff. TV interviews. A new flat. I jumped as someone touched my shoulder.

It was Jonathan. "You okay?"

"Yes, fine. Where's Dad?"

"Looking at the greenhouse. I lent him a measuring tape so he could measure up for some shelves he wants to put up."

I detached myself from the wall. "I'd better get back. I need to book my flight and plan my trip to London. I have to be there by Sunday evening."

"So, it's going ahead then?"

"You mean you thought it wasn't?"

He gave me a lopsided smile. "I was kinda hoping it wouldn't happen. That you would stay, and we would continue this…this thing."

I laughed. "Thing?"

"Yeah." He touched his chest, then mine. "You, me, you know—us."

I turned to look at the water again. "I feel confused about that." I looked at him over my shoulder. "Don't you?"

He nodded. "Yes. I can't even express how I feel about you. I've never felt like this about any woman before. There are so many layers here."

"I know."

"We've got to know each other in a short time."

"Except I thought you were gay at first," I confessed.

He looked at me incredulously. "You did? Why?"

"Just something someone said that I misunderstood. Never mind."

"Well, I'm not gay." He grabbed my waist and pulled me

close. Then he kissed me hard on the mouth and let me go so fast I nearly fell into the river. "Proof enough?"

My lips tingled. "More than enough. Oh, I wish you *were* gay," I blurted out, steadying myself, my hands on the wall behind me. "I mean, when I thought you were gay, it was all so easy. We were dear friends, and I could tell you anything without—"

"—without sex raising its ugly head?" Jonathan laughed. "I had no idea you thought I was gay. So that's why there was such a lack of tension. You treated me like a brother. I was wondering why."

I sighed and looked at my feet, unable to meet his gaze. "I'm sorry. I should have known." I looked up at him and sighed. "I feel horribly confused. I'm glad I'm going away now. We need a little space, don't you think?"

"I suppose. Maybe. I don't know what to say to you. But I'll be busy too. I have a lot of work to catch up on, and I have to go to the dig soon." He took my hand. "Come on, let's go back and let your dad know we're okay. He was worried about you and me. He's also a little conflicted. He doesn't know if he should be happy about your huge career break or sad that you're moving."

"Okay. Let's go back. It's getting dark anyway."

Hand in hand, we wandered slowly back in the gathering dusk, each in our own thoughts. Despite the confusion, I felt a kind of calm settle on my shoulders like a soft silk cape. It would all work out. Eventually. I just had to go out there and see the world first.

CHAPTER 15

I landed at London City Airport the following Sunday. As I had caught a flight from Cork, the transition from country town to big city was mind-blowing. I had been to London a few times before, but it had been a long time since my last visit. Not feeling brave enough to tackle the throng in the Tube, I took a taxi to The Bloomsbury hotel, where Kit's secretary had booked a room.

I checked in, and the porter took my bag and showed me to a room on the second floor. I tipped him and closed the door, eager to inspect my new lodgings. I loved hotel rooms, especially rooms as plush as this one.

Like a child, I bounced on the double bed, took off my shoes, and lay down among the linen-covered pillows, looking up at the ceiling, saying out loud, "I'm in London!" Then I got up and inspected the bathroom, which was huge, with a roll-top bath and shelves stacked with fluffy towels and luxury brand toiletries.

I padded across the soft carpet to the window and peered through the velvet curtains, looking out at the busy street below. I studied the people walking along the pavement, noting the women's clothes and realising how different London fashion was from the countrified styles of Cloughmichael. My pencil skirt and linen jacket suddenly seemed so last year. I needed to update my wardrobe—fast. I checked my watch. Just past lunchtime. Bond Street was fairly near; there must be shops open there even on a Sunday. Or I could take a walk further, to Oxford Street, where I knew I'd find some of my favourite brands.

As I stepped out of the hotel, I was assaulted by the noises and smells of London. The soft, flower-laden breezes and Sunday afternoon peace of Cloughmichael seemed light years away. But despite the din of the traffic and the petrol fumes, there was a buzz in the air that made my heart beat faster and my step lighter. I suddenly knew where to go. Peter Jones, Sloane Square. Not as upmarket as Harrods, and perhaps a bit middle class and middle-aged, but I knew I'd find bargains there. I'd have to brave the Tube and all the different connections, but I told myself that if I was to live in London, I had to get used to it.

I descended into the muggy air of the nearest Tube station, bought an Oyster card, had it loaded with ten trips, and got on the line that would take me to Sloane Square.

The journey took less than ten minutes, and I soon found Peter Jones across the square from the Tube station. So far so good. The square was thronged with tourists and Sunday shoppers, and I was relieved to step into the cool entrance hall of Peter Jones. I breathed in that special department store smell of several perfumes mingled together and looked for the information panel. While I skimmed the different departments, I spotted a sign at the bottom: "Personal shopper available. Enquire at customer services." What a great idea. I found the right desk and asked if there was a personal shopper available.

There was only one on duty that day, Sarah, a beautiful black girl with dreadlocks. She beamed at me with perfect teeth and declared me "the best looking customer in years."

I smiled at her. "Thanks. I need a little help with my wardrobe. I need to get more, uh, fashionable and sleek for a job."

She rubbed her hands together. "Goody. Let's start. What kind of job is it?"

"Editor of a magazine. *The Bluestocking Review*. It's a literary publication."

Sarah looked at me blankly. "Never heard of it. But then again, I'm not that into literature." She looked me up and down. "But that's publishing, right?"

"Sort of, yes."

"Hmm. Okay. *The Bluestocking*—something, you said? Sounds a little boring. But hey, let's give it an edge. What do you say?"

"Sounds good," I replied with only a slight hesitation. "I'm open to all suggestions."

"Fabulous." Her eyes narrowed as she studied me. "I'm thinking slightly eccentric. Sexy boho-chic, perhaps… We'll start with shoes and go on from there. I usually end with shoes, but in your case I want to do something wild."

We started our shopping expedition in the shoe department, where Sarah picked out a pair of sneakers with a band of glitter across the top and pink laces, sandals with stiletto heels, and a pair of ballet flats. Then we went all round the store and picked out skirts, tops, trousers and jackets until we had a pile to bring to the fitting room.

I spent an hour trying everything on, then I picked out a long flowing silk skirt and pink tee shirt Sarah urged me to team with the sneakers, skinny white jeans and a thigh-length loose blouse in a blue and green paisley pattern that would go with the sandals, and a blue, wide-legged trouser suit. I wasn't sure about the sneakers or the skirt, but when I tried them on, I saw they worked perfectly.

All the clothes had a new, edgy cut, some of the hems geometric and some dipping at the back and short at the front. I picked out a few other items I liked and was soon standing at the checkout spending more than a month's rent. Even with the 20 percent off that Sarah fixed for me, it was still a hefty sum. But Kit had said his firm would cover all expenses. I arranged to have my shopping sent to the hotel, thanked Sarah for her help and walked out feeling slightly dazed. But I was ready for my first working day in London.

* * *

After a little sightseeing, I returned to the hotel and ordered room service. I couldn't face the posh dining room on my own. Kit hadn't been in touch, so I assumed he was busy elsewhere. I was all alone in London. But the shopping had been delivered, and I spent a fun half hour trying everything on, mixing and matching the items in all kinds of different ways. Then my dinner arrived, and a waiter rolled in a trolley with a silver cover and half a bottle of Pinot Grigio in a cooler. He whipped off the lid with great flourish and told me to roll the trolley into the corridor when I had finished.

I ate my sole on the bone and sautéed potatoes in front of the enormous flat-screen TV, watching the evening news. After I had rolled the trolley out, I went back into my room, flicking through the channels. Nothing much on. I yawned. Here I was, in a plush hotel in London with nothing to do. I yawned again and went into the bathroom, turned on the taps, and poured in some pink bath salts from the large bottle.

After a blissful half hour, I put on the fluffy white hotel robe and lay on my bed, trying to decide whether to read a book or phone a friend. Phoning a friend seemed the best option. Who would I call? Jonathan? I punched in his number but only got his voicemail. I hung up without leaving a message and scrolled through my contact list. Jules or Miranda? No, they'd be busy on a Sunday evening, but Dessie might like a chat. But before I had a chance to call her, my phone rang from an unknown number.

Intrigued, I swiped the green button. "Hello? Audrey Killian here."

"Hi, Audrey," a faintly familiar voice said. "This is Rory."

I sat up. "Rory? Oh my God, what's happened? Is Dessie okay?"

He laughed. "Yes, she's fine. She asked me to call you to see if you needed anything."

"That's very kind. I need nothing and everything, actually. I'm lonely but excited at the same time. And I have a rather scary week ahead of me. I'm being interviewed on TV, then I have to go and meet my new staff. I also need to find somewhere to live, which, judging by rental prices I've seen online, will be some challenge."

"Sounds like a lot to cope with. But I think I can help you with that last challenge."

"You can?" I said, mystified.

"Yes." He paused. "You see, we have a little pied-à-terre in Fulham. A tiny flat. One room and kitchenette. You couldn't swing that lovely cat of yours in it if you tried. More of a shoebox than a flat, to be honest. Dessie used it during the week when she was working. But now she has taken a year off because of the baby, so we were thinking you might like to rent it."

"For how much?"

"A peppercorn rent. Let's say two hundred a month to cover the charges. Okay with you?"

"Okay?" I laughed. "Are you kidding? It's a lifesaver. Thank you so much. You're both angels from heaven."

"Don't thank me, thank Dessie. I wasn't really keen on the idea, but she talked me into it. I wanted to sell the flat, but she thought we should hang on to it for when she goes back to work. No idea how we're going to organise that. I'd like to see my wife and child here on the farm permanently. But that wouldn't be fair, would it?"

"Don't ask me to even say one word on that subject," I

chortled. "But one step at a time, eh? You never know what the future will bring."

He sighed. "You're right. Anyway, I'm going home to Ireland tomorrow, and I'll be there with Dessie until the baby is born."

"Will you be staying at your old house? I heard it hasn't been sold yet."

"That's old news. Haven't you heard the latest?"

"What?" I asked.

"Finola and Colin bought it. They're coming back to live in Ireland."

"Oh, wow. That's big news. Why didn't anyone tell me?"

Rory laughed. "Aren't you supposed to be telling us? You're the journalist. But anyway, that's what's happening. So we're staying with Jules until the baby is born. Oh, and before you hang up, Dessie said that when you do move to London, you're welcome here in Gloucestershire any weekend you feel like a little country air."

"That'll be wonderful. Thank you. And I'll babysit if you want to go out, after you teach me which way is up on a baby."

"Be careful with such promises. We might take you up on it."

"Please do. I'm hoping I'll have one of my own someday, so it would be good to practise."

"Really?" Rory asked with a laugh. "You have a suitable dad in mind?"

"No, nothing like that," I protested. "I have to look after my career first. But one day, who knows?"

Yes, who knows? I thought when I had hung up. My thoughts drifted to Jonathan. What was he doing right now? Working on his book? I had sent him the first pass of my edits, so he'd have plenty to do. He was a good writer but needed the eagle eye of an editor—someone like me, a real nit-picker. The next editing pass would be even tighter and more detailed.

I yawned and stretched, my eyes closing. Tomorrow would be full of challenges. But I was looking forward to seeing my new office and meeting the staff. That would be fun. I was sure they'd be happy to meet me.

I didn't relish the thought of the interviews, though. Big city reporters—a bunch of bitchy women with sharp pencils and even sharper minds. That would be the worst part of the day.

* * *

I couldn't have been more wrong. The visit to the office of *The Bluestocking Review* in Bloomsbury, just a short walk from the hotel, was a nightmare. Even though Kit had assured me they were "excited to meet their new boss," the hostile atmosphere told a different story.

The office was large and bright, with an open plan layout. Everyone worked in the same room, except for the editor-in-chief, whose office was "at the back," I was told. Standing in the main office, I cleared my throat noisily.

"Excuse me," I called. "I'm Audrey Killian, your new editor-in-chief. I'd just like to say a few words before I meet Majella."

Everyone looked up. "Make it short, please," said a woman with glasses perched on top of her grey hair. "We have a deadline. Majella isn't coming in until after lunch. She never does."

I blinked. "What? But I had an appointment to meet her this morning."

"Well, she must have meant after lunch or something," a tall woman with red hair stated.

I shrugged, trying to look as if it didn't matter. "Oh. Okay. Fine. I'll meet her later, so. This is a grand office anyway."

"Grand?" a voice asked. "Is that the way you talk in good ol' Oireland? Do you come with subtitles?"

There was a brief titter before another voice said, "Come on, Fiona, don't be rude."

"Sorry," Fiona said. "Just joking. No offense."

I smiled stiffly. "None taken. Being Irish is a badge of courage here in London. But I didn't expect to come across prejudice in this office. I've read this magazine every month since I was in my late teens and have always been impressed by the open minds and fair treatment of any author regardless of race or creed. If you have issues with me or my work, let me know, but not if it's just about where I'm from."

Someone started a slow handclap. A young Indian woman at the back stood up. "Majella isn't here, but I can show you her office, which will be yours soon. My name's Malika, by the way."

I nodded. "Thank you, Malika."

"This way," she said, and I followed her into a small room at the back with a window overlooking a concrete courtyard with overflowing rubbish bins.

"Not so lovely," I said, glancing out. "But this desk is nice." I ran my hands over the scarred leather top of the antique mahogany desk, where many editors before me had laboured over manuscripts and books. I turned back to the main office and went to talk to the staff. They all ignored me, working away at their laptops, talking on the phone, or reading documents, whispering to each other.

Giving up on any further communication, I left, feeling both frustrated and upset. How on earth was I going to work with this bunch of snooty bitches? I wasn't looking forward to meeting Majella, but before that, I had the lunch in Chelsea with some journalists Kit's PR manager had organised. Would they eat me alive too?

CHAPTER 16

That was another thing I got wrong. The journalists were a jolly bunch made up of three male reporters and two women. Over a delicious lunch, they fired questions that were both fun and interesting. I responded, cracking jokes and batting the conversational ball back and forth while they tapped my answers down on their tablets. I also posed for photographs in the nearby park, happy I had picked the skinny white pants and loose blouse combo teamed with the sneakers.

Just as we said goodbye, my phone pinged. It was a text message from Majella, who wanted to meet me at the café across the street from the office for afternoon tea. Buoyed up by the success of my press lunch, I set off back to Bloomsbury on the Tube, noting how used I was already to this mode of transport. I was beginning to take to big city life.

Majella was already seated at a table by the window of the café, which was elegantly decorated like a Victorian tea salon. She turned her head as I entered and raised an eyebrow. "Audrey Killian?" she asked in her famous husky voice.

"Yes." I approached, not sure if it was okay to sit down before she had invited me.

Majella gestured to the gilt chair opposite her. "Please. Sit."

I sat, trying not to stare. Majella was tall and blonde with a square jaw and piercing pale blue eyes under black brows. Her hair was cut in a razor-sharp bob, and she was dressed in a black pantsuit with a pink silk scarf flung artfully across her shoulders.

"So," she said when I was seated. "Tea?"

I nodded. "Yes, please."

"Indian? China?"

"Indian, please."

"A pot of Indian, please, Dorothy," Majella said to the waitress who had just appeared. "And some of those delicious scones with clotted cream and jam. Strawberry okay?" she said with a glance in my direction.

"Perfect," I replied, regretting the large lunch that was sitting in my stomach like a lump of concrete. But I didn't dare refuse. There was something about Majella that made you want to agree with everything she said. I stole a glance at her as she checked her phone. She was incredibly well-preserved for a woman of nearly sixty. She didn't look in the slightest like someone who was ready to retire. I jumped as she looked back at me and shot her a cheery smile.

"I hear you were in the office," she said. "Snooping around."

"Snooping? Not really. I thought I would go and meet the staff. I also expected to meet you there. I thought that was arranged."

"By whom? Christopher Montgomery and his crowd? I'm afraid they misled you."

I clasped my hands in my lap. "Oh? Okay. But we're here now. Meeting."

"Indeed."

"Yes." There was a long pause while I desperately tried to think of something intelligent to say. "So," I started as the waitress arrived with our order, "you're retiring?"

Majella spread cream and jam on a scone before she replied. Then she looked at me, her eyes full of disdain.

"Retiring? No, I'm bloody not. That arsehole fired me when he bought our magazine."

"What?" I dropped a big blob of jam on my pants.

"You got jam on those white trousers. That'll never come out."

I dabbed at the red stain with the linen napkin. "I'm sure it will. I'll get some Vanish or something. But never mind that." I looked at her. "He fired you? Why?"

"Because he knew he'd never be able to order me around. He's planning to fire Malika too, because 'she's not quite the type of reviewer we want around here.' His words, not mine. He's a fucking racist and we all know it. He explained he wanted the magazine to review more popular books, like chick lit and romances. Mills and Boon, for fuck's sake! The bloody mass market. And, as the cherry on the cake, he suggested we ask for money in return for a good review. Wouldn't that make us look good? When I said no, he fired me."

The bad language spoken with that cut-glass posh British accent would have made me laugh if it weren't for those revelations.

"He never said anything about this to me," I cut in when Majella drew breath. "He said you were retiring and that he wanted me to run the magazine because he was impressed with the job I was doing on the supplement I created for our own newspaper." I pulled out a folded copy of the latest issue of *Country Weekend* from my bag and put it on the table.

Majella glanced at it. "Charming. Nice photography." She raised her gaze and looked at me. "He told me you have a PhD in English literature."

I nodded. "Yes. That's right."

"What was your thesis about?"

"Women authors in the nineteenth century."

There was a hint of approval in Majella's eyes. "Good for you. Well, that would qualify you in some way, I suppose. You must know that *The Bluestocking Review* was started here in Bloomsbury by some of the daughters of the suffragettes and that we have been growing ever since. We now review all art forms. Film, theatre, music, dance, painting, sculpture, and so on, and we have reviewers all over the country. We're no longer just an avant-garde women's magazine either, but the most important review publication in Britain."

I smiled and nodded. "I know that. I'm a huge fan of the magazine. I read it every month, and I have a big pile of back issues. I buy all my books on the strength of your reviews. You've never been wrong."

Majella inclined her head. "Thank you. I'm glad to hear it." She grabbed the teapot and poured tea into the delicate china cups. "Let's not waste this excellent tea."

I poured a little milk into my cup from the jug. "So tell me, what are you going to do now that you're leaving?"

"I haven't decided yet. I was told I'd have to be gone by the fifteenth of August—only three weeks from today." She smirked. "But I'll think of something. I might even start a rival magazine and poach the staff from you."

I couldn't help laughing. "That would be a great revenge. Not that I'd miss them. They weren't exactly welcoming."

"They probably thought you were in cahoots with Christopher Montgomery. He's not hugely popular with women in London."

"But I'm not," I exclaimed.

"I know that now."

"Must say I'm a little bewildered after what you told me," I continued. "The Montgomery Group owns the newspaper I run in Ireland, you see. We've been working hard to increase circulation and just recently published the magazine. Then I was offered this job, which kind of puzzled me."

"Me too, believe me," Majella said with feeling. "So, who's going to take over from you, then? I bet they have someone in mind already."

"They haven't said anything about that except—" I stopped. "Oh God, Kit said they'd 'take care of it,' when I was having dinner with him and Geoff."

Majella nodded knowingly. "Sure they will. Then they'll fire the whole staff, and before you know it, the newspaper will be all British, and very soon there'll be a political slant creeping in."

My teacup stopped on the way to my mouth. "Political? What do you mean? It's just a little country newspaper."

Majella leaned forward and lowered her voice. "I have heard from some of my reporter friends that there are British Brexiters all over Europe, trying to infiltrate other countries' affairs in order to break up the European Union. Sneaky propaganda by stealth. I bet that's what Montgomery is up to. He's very thick with those neo-Nazi bunch of shits."

I jumped. "What? Neo—"

"Well, you know. Those right-wing populist groups. They hate women too. I'm sure you have them in Ireland as well. Not officially, but closet right-wing racist men in politics."

I suddenly realised she could be onto something. Kit had been mixing with some of the right-wing politicians who went to Killybeg for weekend breaks. I had seen some well-known faces in his golf group, but it hadn't registered with me. Had he been there to network?

Majella's voice cut into my thoughts. "I have a feeling he got rid of you in order to have the coast clear. Then he got you over here and gave you a job you wouldn't refuse, thinking at the same time he'd be able to manipulate you."

"M-manipulate?" I stammered. "How?"

"Sex," Majella hissed. "You do find him sexy, don't you?"

I felt my face go red. "Well, uh, yeah, kind of."

She snorted. "Of course. So do I. The man is sex on legs. If I had no standards, I would have had a little fling with him myself, just for fun. Don't tell me it hasn't crossed your mind."

"Yeah, well, sure it has. I'm only human."

She nodded, looking satisfied. "There you go. He'd prob-ably have you in his bed sooner or later. I have to tell you that he's been fooling around with women and threatened those who didn't respond to his advances. He's a vindictive, dangerous man."

I coughed, a bit of scone stuck in my throat. "Oh, come on," I protested. "That's a bit over the top, isn't it?"

Stony faced, Majella glared back at me. "Believe me, the man's a monster. He eats women journalists for breakfast."

"Murdoch is suddenly looking like a pussycat compared to him," I quipped.

Majella threw her head back and laughed. "Priceless. You're right." She raised her teacup. "But I have a plan. I didn't think I could realise it until I had this chat with you. But together I think we might be able to beat that creep at his own game. If only we had a little more ammunition. But we can bide our time. Here's to the power of women."

I laughed and clinked my cup against hers. "Cheers, Majella. We'll get them. The mills of God and all that."

"One day they'll grind them all, eh?"

I grinned "Definitely."

* * *

That extra ammunition Majella had been wishing for pre-sented itself later that afternoon.

My mind reeling after our meeting, I made my way on foot back to the hotel. As I walked across the marble floor of the lobby, a woman approached me.

"Excuse me, but are you Audrey Killian?" she said in an accent that was unmistakably Irish.

Startled, I turned and looked at her. "Yes. How did you know my name?"

"I recognised you from the photo in your magazine. The editorial column." She gestured at the copy of *Country Weekend* I had stuck under my arm.

"Oh. I see."

She held out her hand and smiled. "I'm Clare Tobin. Assistant manager of Keatings. We had some dealing with your publication recently."

"Ah, yes," I said, shaking her hand. "That was a pity. But we couldn't afford the big discount you wanted."

The woman looked confused. "Big discount? We wanted 30 percent. That was quite generous, we thought. But then the publisher was in touch and said the deal was off because you wouldn't be able to meet the orders of a countrywide distribution."

My jaw dropped. "What? There must be some mistake. We would have managed that without a problem. We were even negotiating with a printing firm that would have…" I stopped, realising what had been going on. Kit had killed the deal so I'd take the job in London. He knew that if *Country Weekend* had been about to become a national magazine, I would never have left. Shit. Majella was right.

"But now we have good news," the woman continued as if she hadn't noticed my confusion. "We have a new deal, I just heard. The Montgomery Group changed their minds and accepted our terms. *The Knockmealdown News* along with the weekend supplement will be going out to our shops all over Ireland by the end of August."

"Really?" I said, trying to focus on what she was saying. "Well, good for them. I won't be working there anymore by then, as I'm taking up a new position here in London."

"Oh. I see. Well, good luck with your new job. Working in London will be exciting. I'm only here for a few days' city break with my husband. Wonderful city, don't you think?"

"Fabulous," I managed. We said goodbye, and I continued to my room, where I was confronted by a large bunch of deep red roses on the table by the window.

I looked at the card and read: *Congratulations on a successful first day in London. Dinner's on me tonight at the Celeste in Belgravia. A taxi will pick you up at seven. Can't wait to see you. Kit xx*

I closed my eyes for a moment. What should I do? Still trying to understand what had happened in connection with Keatings, I wondered if I should call and cancel. But that would only push the confrontation forward. I decided to call Majella for advice.

"Roses and a dinner date at Celeste? He's really keen to get you on his side. And into his bed," she added with a dirty cackle

"I know," I moaned. "What should I do? Cancel?"

"Never," Majella snapped. "Quite the opposite. Not that you have much on him right now, though."

"Oh, but I do," I said and told her about the conversation with the woman from Keatings.

Majella started to laugh. "Of course! What did I tell you? Once you're out of the way and he has his new editor, they can start slipping in their propaganda. How incredible that you bumped into her. That's what I call great good fortune. Not that I know how we can use it, though."

I smiled, a plan forming in my mind. "I think I can come up with something."

"What?"

"I'll tell you later."

"Right, but be careful. And reel him in slowly, like a fish. Let him think all is okay. Do your wide-eyed Bambi look and pretend to be impressed."

"Wide-eyed Bambi look?" I said.

"Come on, darling," Majella drawled. "Don't pretend you don't do that sometimes."

"Uh, okay, maybe. Occasionally."

"That's my girl. Dress to kill and go get 'em."

I let out a giggle. "I'll do my best. I'll call you later with a report." I hung up and threw myself on the bed, drawing up a plan for the evening ahead. I had plenty of ammunition, but I needed more, just to be sure, and I knew where I might get it. I looked up Rory's number.

He answered on the first ring. "Audrey? What's up?"

"Nothing, I just wanted to ask you a question, as you used to be in politics."

"Politics? Yes, I was. But I'm trying my best to forget it."

"Try to remember a little bit right now. What do you know about John McCullough, Dermot Ryan and… Shit, I forgot the last one. Something Donnelly?"

"Brian Donnelly," Rory filled in, sounding cross. "Those three are known operators. Members of the Irish Parliament who are trying to start a debate about Ireland leaving the EU. Little shits all of them. Why do you ask?"

"I saw them at Killybeg with…someone. Never mind. Forget I asked. Thanks a million, Rory. See you soon in Ireland."

"You're welcome. You'll tell me what this is all about soon, I hope?"

"I will. When it's safe."

CHAPTER 17

Dressed to kill in a slinky black dress, sandals with stiletto heels and my hair swept up, I fine-tuned my campaign in the taxi that had pulled up in front of the hotel on the dot of seven. The trip to the restaurant in posh Belgravia took twenty minutes through heavy traffic.

Feeling slightly wobbly, I stepped into the discreetly lit plush restaurant. I only had to give Kit's name to the maître d' before he ushered me to a table beside the window, through which I could glimpse the lights snaking along the Thames in the velvety night. Kit rose and kissed my cheek while the waiter fussed around me, placing a napkin in my lap, pouring water, and handing me the menu. There was the quiet murmur of a very exclusive and expensive restaurant and the smell of Michelin-star food.

We looked at each other across the table when all was calm again. I smiled, feeling like an actress about to play the role of her life—or a double agent risking everything to save her country. "Hi there," I purred. "Nice to see you."

"Hell, you're beautiful," Kit said. "There's a glow to you tonight. Is it the new job?"

I smiled. "Maybe just the excitement of the big city. Thank you for the flowers, by the way."

"Glad you liked them." His eyes drifted from my face to my cleavage. "Nice dress. New?"

"Yes. I got a pile of stuff at Peter Jones today. Expensive, but as you said you'd cover any expenses, I sent the invoice to your accountant. Hope you don't mind."

"Of course not, darling. It's well worth it."

"Thank you." I turned my attention to the menu. "I think I'll have the lobster and a salad. I don't feel like a heavy meal. I'm rather stuffed after all I ate today."

Kit nodded. "I'll have the same. A full stomach would ruin the rest of the evening," he added with a slow smile. He gestured to a waiter and made the order, adding a bottle of Bollinger—"to celebrate."

How fecking obvious, I thought as I tried to look excited. *But we'll soon pour cold water on that.* "Fabulous," I chirped.

"Good day?" he asked.

"Very. But a bit tiring. I met my new staff this morning, then I had the press lunch, and then—" I paused "—I had tea with Majella."

His eyes widened. "You did? But I thought she wasn't keen on seeing you. Or something," he ended. Did he look suddenly pale?

"She wasn't really. But we got on fine."

The colour came back to his cheeks. "Oh. Good. What did you talk about?"

I took a sip of water and reached for a bread roll. "Nothing much. She filled me in on her future plans and told me a little bit about the magazine. Then we just chatted about this and that. You know, girl stuff."

"Oh. I see." He let out a sound as if he'd been holding his breath. "Girl stuff, eh?"

I smiled innocently. "Yeah. She's nice."

Kit looked startled. "Nice? Majella? Never heard anyone say that." He took out his handkerchief and wiped his forehead. "A bit hot in here, isn't it?"

"I find it perfect. But then, I'm wearing a lot less than you in that suit."

His gaze skimmed my body. "So you are."

I looked at him, realising that where before I'd have found that look very hot, I no longer did. He only seemed pathetic and sleazy. What had I been thinking?

The champagne arrived in a cooler and was expertly opened by the sommelier. When we each had a brimming glass, I raised mine. "Cheers, Kit. Thanks for inviting me to this amazing restaurant."

Kit raised his glass. "Cheers, sweetheart. Welcome to London. We'll have lots of fun, I promise."

I put down my glass and decided to launch my attack. "I'm sure we will. But I have to go back tomorrow and sort things out with *The Knockmealdown News* first."

He cleared his throat. "Yes, that's true."

"I want to appoint Dan as editor. He's very—"

"I don't think he'd be up to the job."

"You just don't know him," I argued. "But okay, maybe not him. Finola McGee's coming back to Cloughmichael, I heard. Maybe she'd like her old job back?"

"I wouldn't hire her. Too opinionated and rebellious."

"Oh?" I widened my eyes. "You want someone softer, more pliable?"

Kit interrupted me. "Look, I have something to tell you. I'm appointing an editor from London to take over. She's very experienced and will run the paper like clockwork. I also want to see a more serious tone in the paper. More about what's happening in the world. So there'll be a political column very soon."

"And Finola McGee, the best political reporter in Ireland wouldn't be able to do that?" I asked, my voice dripping with sarcasm.

"No. She'd be too…too controversial."

I stared at him. "Really? And what would be wrong with that?" I paused when the waiters arrived with our lobsters. "Looks divine," I cooed and picked up my lobster fork. "Mmm, gorgeous," I mumbled through my mouthful.

He put a small piece of lobster into his mouth and chewed without enthusiasm. "So you have no objection? To my appointing a UK editor, I mean."

I put down my fork. Time to go for the jugular. "Objection?" I said, lifting an eyebrow. "I don't feel I can comment, as I'm supposed to be leaving. But I know exactly what kind of shite you're up to, and I don't like it."

"What do you mean? Up to?" he asked, a note of annoyance in his voice.

I took a swig of champagne to steady my nerves. Then I put both hands on the table and fixed him with my eyes. "Kit," I said in a voice so low he had to lean forward to hear me. "I just found out what you've been doing behind my back. I happened to bump into a woman from Keatings earlier today. She gave me some very interesting information."

Kit, his face red, inhaled, as if to say something.

I held up my hand. "Shut up," I said quietly, "or everyone in the restaurant will hear me."

"Okay," he muttered. "So talk."

"Majella also filled me in on the circumstances of her so-called retirement. I won't bore you with the details, but all I've seen so far of this rather unsavoury stew is making me sick. So—" I paused for effect, feeling an odd tingle of excitement as I saw the fear in his eyes. I had him.

"So…?" he wheezed.

"So, I want my old job back. I want a raise for everyone in the office too." I smiled sweetly. "I also think you should rehire Majella."

"Why should I? She's a bitch."

"And you're a gobshite. If you don't agree, I'll accuse you of sexual harassment and make it very public."

"You have no proof."

"No? What about all those saucy text messages you sent me? I would qualify that as 'sexting,' actually. I saved them all. Including the one about you firing me if I didn't sleep with you, accompanied by—" I winked "—some rather revealing pictures."

"That was meant as a joke. I thought it'd turn you on."

"It doesn't look like a joke. And no, it didn't. Nothing about you turns me on. Not even a close-up of you-know-what. So, yeah, I have some pretty good evidence right there."

"That accusation will wear very thin in court."

I laughed and picked up another piece of lobster. "What court? I'll paste it all over the Internet. Much cheaper and a lot more fun. Facebook, Twitter, Instagram, and hey, why not Pinterest too? The suffragettes out there will eat you alive."

"I'll deny it and sue you."

I shook my head. "Come on, Kit, you know how it works. The story will be out there. Denying it and suing me will only make it worse. Mud sticks, you know."

Kit's face turned a sickly shade of green. "So, you're not going to accept the position here after all? And you want your old job back, or you'll paste my—all over the Internet?"

"You got it."

He looked at me with such hatred I winced. "Very well. You've got me cornered. But what do I do about the press release? And the interviews? That's all due to go out tomorrow."

"There's plenty of time to stop that. Just a couple of phone calls will do it."

"It'll make us look really bad. They'll think something's up."

"And wouldn't they be right? But I'm sure you can think of a plausible lie to tell them. You're good at that. Lying, I mean." I paused and then fired the next and final bullet. "I also found out who you've been networking with at Killybeg—a bunch of Irish Euro sceptics. Golf partners you said? More like partners in crime. Or politics, which to me is the same thing. But of course, that detail is nothing I can prove. You'd replace me with a British editor-in-chief, you said?"

"That was the plan."

"And then, one by one you'd fire everybody on the staff and replace them too, right? With little Brexiters who will sneak in propaganda and spread it all around."

Kit blanched. "I don't know what you're talking about."

I rolled my eyes. "Sure you don't. But that's not going to happen now, thank goodness." I got up. "I'm leaving now. I'll be going back to Ireland tomorrow to get back to work. I'll be busy if we're to meet the new orders that Keatings will be placing."

Kit stared at me, his eyes full of venom. "I'm seriously thinking of closing that paper down."

I waved my phone at him. "You might be sorry," I chanted.

"I might sell it. There's this new publishing group that has been expressing an interest. They might be tougher to deal with than me."

"Maybe they'll be more professional. But whatever. I'm off." I pushed my chair under the table. "Please don't get up. I'll see myself out. Thanks for dinner. It was truly delicious."

He didn't reply. I waggled my fingers at him and walked out, nodding to the waiter and telling the maître d' that Mr Montgomery would like his bill and could he please get me a taxi. I shivered as I stood on the pavement despite the warm air. I had won the battle, but what about the war?

* * *

I checked out of the hotel that evening. The receptionist presented me with a bill for close to a thousand pounds.

"But the Montgomery Group said they'd pay my hotel bill," I protested.

The girl gave me a cold stare. "We just had a call from them to say you'd have to settle the bill yourself."

"Oh." I gritted my teeth and gave her my credit card, knowing my account would be stripped to the last cent. I'd have to ask Dad for a loan.

I left the hotel and found a room at a small bed and breakfast near the airport. I didn't want Kit or any of his thugs to find me. When I was finally tucked into bed, I called Majella and gave her the good news.

"You did it!" she whooped. "Christ, you're good. Do you want a job? I could do with someone like you on my team."

"Thanks, but I want to go back home and sort things out. Don't think I should come back to London for a while anyway."

"The offer will still stand if you change your mind. Can't make you editor-in-chief, but you can be my assistant or something when I get my magazine back. If he doesn't sell it from under me, of course."

I turned in the bed, trying to make myself comfortable on the lumpy mattress. "He won't. It makes too much money. So you're stuck with him. But I doubt he'll get involved in what you do. He's such a chickenshit deep down."

I hung up after having said goodnight and promised to be in touch next time I was in London. I snuggled under the polyester sheets and tried to go to sleep, happy at the thought of going home. But what a mess I had created. It would take a lot of work to clear it all up.

* * *

The heatwave broke the next morning. I arrived at Cork Airport after a bumpy flight, stepping onto the tarmac in heavy rain. I scurried into the terminal as fast as I could but still managed to get soaked to the skin. Dad was there to meet me. He threw his rain mac across my shoulders as we made our way to the parking lot and his car. We hurried to load my suitcase into the boot and got into the car, laughing as we banged the doors shut.

"Phew," I exclaimed and grabbed an old cardigan from the back seat to dry my hair. "That's some rainstorm."

Dad dabbed his face with a hanky. "The weather changed about an hour ago. It was rather a wild drive here." He grinned. "Great to have you back, if only for a few weeks. How was your trip?"

"Eventful," I said, wondering if I should break the news to him then or wait until we were back in Cloughmichael. "I'll tell you later, when we're home."

He nodded, his eyes on the road and the heavy rain. "Yes, we can talk then. This rain makes it hard to drive."

"Back to a normal Irish summer, then." I sighed, pulled the rain mac tighter around me, and turned up the heat.

Dad glanced at me. "We'll be home soon. I got some soup and fresh bread for lunch. Sorry, that was all I could think of. I'm no cook, as you know. I would have asked Jonathan, but he has some visitor with him. A very cute woman, actually. Maybe he has a girlfriend."

"What did you say?" I asked, wondering if I had misheard through the drumming of the rain and the sound of the heater.

"Girlfriend," Dad shouted. "Jonathan—maybe he has one." He shot a sideways look at me. "Sorry, didn't mean to upset you. You weren't…you and him, I mean?"

"No, we're just friends," I said and looked out at the rainswept landscape. I bit my lip hard to stop the tears that threatened to well up. It couldn't be true. Jonathan had hinted at deep feelings for me, but we had, without saying it, come to an understanding to keep things cool for a while. At least those were the vibes I got before I left. I'd probably read it all wrong.

Another failed relationship before it even started. I was probably doomed to be single for the rest of my life—just like Majella and all the other successful career women. What was it Miranda said? That in order for love to last, you have to give up a piece of yourself? That's what Jules had done and Pandora too. And they were happy having done it. I closed my eyes. It was hard to accept. But it was there, and it was true. I shook my head to clear my mind. Love and feelings were too confusing right now. I had to sort out the office and the future of the paper.

"Jerry had some good news," Dad said, his voice cutting into my daydream. "The insurance company agreed to pay the full value of the house. The fire was caused by a faulty router. So it wasn't your fault after all."

"That's a relief."

"It was considered an accident. So both your boss and Jerry will get compensation. He's going to rebuild and make it more modern inside. *The Knockmealdown News* can move back in less than a year."

"Great news. Jerry must be happy, even if he doesn't own the paper anymore. But it's still part of him."

"Very much so. I met him at the pub down the road one evening. Liz introduced us. We had a long chat over some good beer. He's a good lad."

"Yes, he is. I'm sure he's sorry he sold the paper to the Montgomery Group, but he had no choice."

"No, he didn't—then," Dad said.

"What?"

Dad winked. "I'll tell you later."

"Tell me what?"

"You'll see."

"Come on, tell me now. What have you been up to?"

But Dad didn't reply. He drove the last few miles humming a little tune, looking very pleased with himself. I knew it was useless to ask any further questions, and I had other things on my mind.

CHAPTER 18

I only gave myself time to change and have some soup before I went upstairs to the office. My flat was in disarray, with tools and planks on the living room floor for "extra shelves" Dad explained before he left to get back to Abbeyleix and the bank. Cat was hiding in my wardrobe, where she glared at me from a pile of cashmere sweaters she had pulled down and settled on as if she were paying me back for having been away. I left her there and ventured upstairs to answer all the questions I knew would come.

I glanced at Jonathan's door, wishing I could see through it. Was he in there with—her? If only he were gay like I thought at first. Then we could keep the lovely friendship, and I wouldn't feel the painful stab of jealousy as I thought of him with another woman. But as always, I pushed away the pain and turned my mind to work and future projects. The paper was going well and would now be sold nationwide. I had beaten Kit into submission. A great victory.

I opened the door to the office and was met by excited chatter. Everyone was gathered around Mary's desk and the big screen, where a number of photos flicked past in quick succession. The weight loss feature had been launched while I was away.

"Hi!" I shouted. "I'm back!"

They all whirled around. "Hi, Audrey," Mary said and

laughed. "Sorry, we were looking at the pictures from the launch. That was such a blast. Pandora organised a fantastic party and we were all in our swimsuits and had champagne around the pool."

"Sounds fabulous." I went to look at the pictures, smiling at the one of Dan looking embarrassed in a pair of navy swimming shorts, his white belly flopping over the top.

"How was London?" Fidelma asked.

"I bet you're dying to get back," Sinead remarked. "Cloughmichael will seem very boring compared to London."

"Did you find a flat yet?" Mary asked. "Is the office huge? Are the women there really glamorous? Did you get interviewed on TV?"

"I bet you were wined and dined by that sexy publisher," Sinead said, her eyes sparkling. "Come on, let's have a coffee and you can tell us all."

"Coffee sounds great." I perched on the edge of the desk. "But before you get excited, I have to tell you something important. Things have changed. I'm not leaving."

They all stared at me. "Come on, stop messing, Audrey," Fidelma said. "We know you're all set to take up that glam job."

I shook my head. "I'm not doing it after all. I turned it down." I folded my arms and looked at them. "I found out a few things about my sudden rise to fame and how it was all a kind of scam. I won't go into the details, but I'll just say I realised that working here at *The Knockmealdown News* is the best job for me. Okay, so maybe being the boss at *The Bluestocking Review* seemed like a dream come true at first, but the reality wasn't as pretty. I'm not good at intrigue and dirty dealings and such things. I just want to stay here and work with you."

"Aww," Mary said. "That's lovely, Audrey. But we're okay. Dan will look after us and run the paper. Isn't that what you agreed with your man?"

"No, it isn't. It was my suggestion, but he didn't agree." I was interrupted by Dan coming into the office with a bag of donuts.

His face fell when he saw me. "Oh. You're back."

I nipped the bag out of his hand. "Yes, and I'm confiscating these. Not part of the new eating plan, are they?"

Dan's face turned pink. "They weren't for me, they were for the girls."

I pulled a donut out of the bag and took a bite. "Lovely. Thank you. Just what I needed. Could we have some coffee and then get to work on that feature?"

He looked at me like a rabbit caught in the headlights. "But I thought… I mean, didn't you say I'd be in charge?"

I nodded and took another bite of donut. "I did, but now I'm back. I'm not moving to London after all. Good news, don't you think?"

He looked longingly at my donut. "Brilliant."

Sinead snorted a laugh. "Yeah, right. Dan's been lording it over us since you left. So we sent him out for donuts."

I put my hand on his shoulder. "But he's still our star photographer."

Dan looked mollified. "That's what I love to do the most too." He sighed. "I'm glad you're back, Audrey, honest. I woulda run the paper the best I could, but the pressure was kinda getting to me all the same. Now I can keep taking pictures and not have to worry."

"It's lonely at the top," Fidelma said, nodding wisely.

I had to laugh. I waved the last of my donut in the air. "Come on, gang, make coffee and let's get to work. Today's Tuesday, we have to do the online paper and then the layout for the magazine. It'll soon be sold in all the Keatings shops all over the country, so we have to pull up our socks and do our best."

"Keatings?" Dan asked. "Are you serious?"

I nodded. "Absolutely. The deal has just been agreed."

"Wow," Mary whispered. "That's incredible."

"And," I continued, "we'll be moving back to the old address as soon as the building has been restored. Won't be for about a year or so, but we'll have our office back."

"Yay," Fidelma cheered. "Not that I don't like it here, but it's a bit cramped and a long hack to this part of town every morning."

None of this had been cleared with either Jerry or Kit, who hadn't been in touch since I marched out of that posh restaurant. But saying it out loud made me feel it was all going to happen. We worked on the feature and the online paper for the following day's issue until late afternoon, and then I told everyone they could go home.

"Anything happen while I was away?" I asked before they left.

"Nothing much," Fidelma said. "Except that Finola McGee and Colin are moving back to Cloughmichael."

Mary nodded. "Yes, and they're buying the old Quirke place and turning it into a mansion."

I put my coffee mug on the desk. "I know. Rory told me."

"Maybe we could do a feature on them?" Dan suggested.

"Great idea," I said. "I'll get in touch when she's here."

I stayed behind and tidied everything up, reading through the piece about the "Fit for Life" launch. It would be a regular feature in the magazine, with tips on healthy eating, exercise, and other items on the subject. I was happy I had agreed that Pandora would slant the whole idea toward health rather than the body beautiful. That would go down better with most people and seemed very inspirational. I flicked through Jonathan's article for the "Romance Through History" feature. No surprise that it was very well written, but I was startled by the stark emotion that came through. He was more romantic than I had thought. I sighed and turned off the computer. No need to make myself sad.

I locked up and went downstairs. Just as I was about to

open my door, there was a clatter of feet on the stairs behind me. I turned around and discovered a woman with red curly hair dressed in jeans and a pink tee shirt. With her green eyes and a face full of freckles, she was attractive in a kooky way.

She stopped and hitched her large tote higher on her shoulder. "Oh, hi. You must be Audrey Killian." She held out her hand. "I'm Clodagh and I—" She was interrupted by a shrill ringtone from her bag. "Shit, my phone. Hang on." She pulled out the phone and answered. "Hi, what's up? Oh no. That's terrible. Could be a fuse, though. But I'll be there as soon as I can. Don't touch anything. Bye." She put the phone back and looked at me. "Sorry. Emergency. Must go. I'll see you soon, right?"

I nodded. "Uh, okay."

She ran out the door without saying goodbye, leaving me standing there, looking at the door banging shut, feeling as if I'd been hit by a hurricane. So that was the girlfriend. Odd woman. But pretty and obviously very fit. I jumped as a voice called my name. Jonathan coming down the stairs.

"You're back," he said and enveloped me in a bear hug. "How did it go?"

I closed my eyes and breathed in the clean smell of lavender soap from his shirt and lingered in his arms for a moment to enjoy the feel of his body and his breath in my hair. Then I pulled away. "Fine. In an odd way."

"Oh?" He looked at me with laughter in his hazel eyes. "You have to tell me. Sorry I wasn't here when you arrived. I've been a little busy."

"So I gather," I said, trying to keep the emotion out of my voice. "I just met…Clodagh. Briefly. She ran out of here as if her pants were on fire."

He laughed. "Yeah. A bit of a whirlwind, isn't she? I meant to tell you about her before you left. But there wasn't time. Maybe you're free tonight? I could cook you dinner if you

want. And you can tell me about London, and I'll explain…
well, Clodagh and what we've decided."

I glared at him. "What do you mean? Dinner with you?
No thank you. I don't need any explanations. It's very clear
what's going on."

He looked startled. "It is?"

"Yes. So save the excuses and everything else." I went
inside and banged the door in his face.

I stumbled on the planks and tools Dad had left in the
living room, swearing loudly. Then I ran into my bedroom,
collapsed on the bed, and burst into tears. I lay there crying
into the pillows while Cat trampled around me, putting a
paw on my face, and finally snuggling into me, as if she were
trying to comfort me. I hugged her tight, and she put up
with it for a while before she wrenched free and ran out of
the room. I lay there, staring into space, tears running into
the pillow, trying to understand what had happened, why
Jonathan had turned to someone else in such a short time.
I had only been gone a few days, and he already had a new
girlfriend? How could I have been so wrong about him and
our relationship? Or had I read too much into what was
only a friendship? That kiss before I left—was that only a
way of showing me he wasn't gay? I couldn't understand it,
no matter how I turned it round and round. We had spent a
lot of time talking, but as I cast my mind back to those evenings, I realised that most of it had been about me. He hadn't
shared much about his own life. All this time I'd thought we
were close. But now it dawned on me that I didn't know him
at all.

CHAPTER 19

I coped with my heartache the only way I knew: by burying myself in work. In any case, Finola's homecoming dominated the gossip the following weeks, which helped take my mind off Jonathan. He seemed to have vanished after that night when I slammed the door in his face. Liz told me he had gone back to the dig in County Meath, as it was starting up again. I didn't know if that was a good thing. I missed him but felt that the space his absence provided was a good thing.

Finola's much anticipated return even spilled into the magazine, as we did a feature on her with an exclusive interview. She provided pictures of the big house they were selling in Malibu. The feature was perfect for the first nationwide issue, which went on to sell "like hotcakes" we were told by a delighted Keatings representative. "Keep it coming, lads," they said in capital letters in an e-mail. So we did.

We asked if we could get an exclusive on the new house too, but Finola refused. That was something she didn't want to broadcast to the nation. "We're putting so much into that house," she told us. "But we want to keep a low profile in Cloughmichael. And there's the security to take into consideration too. Plus, the girls will be going to a local school. We want to give them a normal life and no celebrity status. It'll wreck them for ever."

Then she came back, and the town buzzed even more, as Colin appeared a few days later, driving from Shannon in a brand-new Volvo SUV. They had to cram into the cottage on Jules' estate while the work was done on the new house. I wondered how they could fit two lively little girls, a nanny, a dog, and a huge pile of luggage into the tiny two-bedroom house. But they had done it before, so they were probably used to it. Jules' main house, although a large manor house, already had Rory and Dessie staying there. The cottage was a better option for Finola's menagerie.

"It's a bit of a squeeze," Finola admitted. "But it's summer, so we're outside most of the time. Thank God for this weather."

She popped into the office one day and caused a minor riot, as everyone crowded around her asking questions and telling her what had been going on since she left.

"Oh God, I miss this," she said as she perched on the edge of Mary's desk.

"This—what?" I asked.

"This." She waved her coffee mug around to encompass the whole office. "I mean the challenge of running a newspaper, getting stories, putting it all together, and then seeing it read everywhere in town. It was the most enjoyable part of my working life." She sighed and drained her mug. "But you can't go back, can you?"

"Is that a question?" I asked, feeling suddenly worried. Finola was the star reporter who had landed in this town and made the newspaper what it was today—except for the magazine. Did she want her job back?

"Nah, it was a statement." Finola got off the desk. "Got to go back. Colin's minding the kids and trying to read a screenplay at the same time."

"I thought you had a nanny," Mary said.

"She quit." Finola shrugged. "Sleeping on the couch kind of lost its appeal after a couple of nights. So she ran back to her mammy in Dublin. But I don't mind. I think nannies are overrated, to be honest. I want to look after my own children from now on, with the help of the occasional babysitter."

Later, I had a chance to talk to Finola privately as I walked her to her car.

"I'm glad to see you back," I said. "I'm sure you'll be happy here. I sure am. I love this town and the people in it."

She stopped walking and looked at me, her eyes narrowing. "Is that why you didn't take that super job in London? Most people would kill for that chance."

"It came with too many strings. Someone was playing dirty tricks."

She leaned against her car, dangling the key in her hand. "By 'someone,' I'm guessing the publisher, right?"

I nodded and stared at my feet. "Well, yes. I couldn't cope with it. I could have stayed, taken the job, and fought for my rights and my career. But it was too big for me to handle." I looked Finola in the eye. "I couldn't let *The Knockmealdown News* be taken over like that. It was all about politics and manipulation. It would have wrecked the paper and hurt a lot of people. I know the new publisher might be worse, but at least I'll be here to fight them and not in London." I drew breath.

"New publisher?"

"Yes. The Montgomery Group are selling *The Knockmealdown News.*"

"To whom?"

I shrugged. "No idea. But whoever they are, I'll be here to defend all we've worked for."

She nodded. "You're right. You might not know who they are yet, but they'll have to show their faces sooner or later." She winked. "But I think I'll have a little snoop here and there and see if I can get any clues. I've nearly finished the first draft of my book about the American elections—a kind of analysis. But I'm only dying to get back into reporting again. I might try to see if I can get some kind of column going somewhere," she added with a wistful look in her eyes. Was she hinting at something? Maybe she was angling to take over my job? But where would that put me? Back working for her? No way.

I straightened my back and folded my arms. "I hope you do. But the office here is kind of crowded as it is. And with this situation going on, I'm not sure—"

Finola threw back her head laughed out loud. "Jesus, woman, I'm not after your job. Calm down." She put her hand on my arm. "We were such a team, weren't we? But you're doing an even better job without me. You're so grounded here, so part of the town and the people, more than I could ever be. You'll have to stay."

"Oh. Thank you." I relaxed my arms and let out my breath.

Finola was still laughing. "You thought I was going to muscle in here and push you out? You silly woman."

"Yeah, I know. Sorry."

"No problem, girl." She punched me playfully on the arm. "I'd better get going, if I can get this old yoke to start." She patted the top of her Mini Cooper Roadster, once her pride and joy, bought with the money from her first book. "Another old friend from my chequered past." She got in and wound down the window. "I'll keep you posted on any news about that illusive publisher."

"If you can find any."

"I will, trust me. I'm Finola McGee, super sleuth, ya know." She revved the engine and drove off with a roar.

I watched the little sports car screech around the corner and felt a glimmer of hope. Finola was sure to dig up something, she always did. I only hoped it would be good rather than bad.

* * *

There were more developments later that day. Kit called and confirmed in curt tones he was selling the paper and already had a bidder. "Some publishing group that has just started up. The Jersean Group. Never heard of them. Have you?"

"No," I replied, nodding at Mary across the desk in my office. "Jersean? Are they based in Jersey?"

"No, they're Irish. Their representative said they've just started up and will be buying some other country newspapers. They want to make Irish country journalism Irish again, she said, whatever that means. Could be a political stunt. So that might land you in more shit than you thought you had with us," he continued with glee in his voice.

"That's impossible," I countered.

He didn't rise to the bait. "I haven't accepted their offer yet. We're negotiating a deal. If that doesn't work, you might find yourself stuck with me. But the paper's still up for sale."

"Why are you selling? I thought you might make more money now as we're in with Keatings."

"No guarantee it'll help sales. The magazine could bomb countrywide. In any case, I'm beginning to find you and the whole scene irritating. The other editors are a lot easier to work with."

"Bigger fish to fry elsewhere, eh?" I quipped. "But you're on to a loser there, my friend. I'll be going to a lot of trade fairs and press events. Interesting how you can get rumours to fly by just a hint here and there."

"You'll be spreading lies about us among your colleagues, is that it?"

I laughed. "No, Kit, I'll be telling the truth."

"Is that a threat?"

"No, it's a promise. If there's nothing else, I'll let you go. I have a magazine to get out, you know."

He hung up without saying goodbye.

I winked at Mary. "What a grump. Where were we?"

"Who was that?"

"My ex-boss. The new one couldn't possibly be worse."

"You never know," Mary said darkly. "New bosses usually have new brooms. I hope they won't sweep us all away."

CHAPTER 20

I tried to push away my worries as we worked on the next issue of the magazine, the second one that would go out nationwide. It would have to be sensational for it to succeed. I had a brief chat with Finola to tell her the name of the new publishing group.

"Jersean?" she said. "How do you spell that?"

"Like it sounds. J-e-r-s-e-a-n."

"Odd name. Never heard of them. But I'll do some research and get back to you if I find anything."

I had delayed telling Dad about my change of plan. But I knew I had to break it to him before anyone else did. I dragged my heels about it until I realised he had to know before he sold his house in Abbeyleix.

"Dad," I said when we were in the garden sharing a pizza and a beer at the table under the trees. "I have something to tell you."

"What?" He shook the table. "This needs fixing. I have my tools in the car. Why didn't you tell me how wobbly it was?"

"I forgot. Are you listening?"

He let go of the table and looked at me. "Yes. What is it? You look worried."

"It's about that job in London. I'm not taking it."

He stared at me. "What? You're not taking it?"

"No."

"Are you mad? After all the hard work, all the—" He stopped and pushed his hand through his hair. "Why are you throwing away this chance? Why are you taking the easy option? Sure, London is a big place, and things will be tough for a while but, hell, Audrey, you have to go for it sometimes. I thought you had more guts than this."

"Stop for a moment," I exclaimed, close to tears. "Just stop. Please don't say anything before I've explained."

He sighed and nodded. "Go on. This had better be good."

"Don't look so angry, Dad. I was so excited about that job, you know. My big break. Working in London at such a prestigious magazine. And you being so happy and proud. But then I found out that I had been offered it as part of a dirty conspiracy to get me out of the way in order to—" I stopped.

"In order to—what?"

"To manipulate me in some way. The whole thing is so off the wall, it sounds crazy. I won't go into the details. Too complicated. It has to do with a lot of things that I find hard to talk about. But the gist of it is that I'm back, I'm staying and—" I smiled "—I'm happy." I took a deep breath and looked at the expression on Dad's face, which had changed from disappointment to anger during my little speech. "I know you're upset. I'm really sorry if you're disappointed in me. You wanted me to have this big career and make loads of money and have my name on the rich list or something. I never understood why, though."

Dad sighed and looked at his plate. "It's because of Patricia—your mum."

"Mum? What does she have to do with it?"

Dad poked at his pizza with his fork. Then he looked at me with eyes so sad it made my heart ache. "She had a great future ahead of her when we met. She was only twenty-two and had just graduated from Trinity with a master's in chemistry. Immediately after that she landed a job with an American pharmaceutical company based in London. It would have been the first rung on the ladder of a career in that field. But then we met and had this whirlwind romance—well, you know how beautiful she was."

"And you were gorgeous. I've seen the photos."

He smiled wistfully. "Yeah, we were a grand-looking pair all right. I had just been promoted at the bank, and then we got married very soon after we met. Pat got pregnant with you, and I got a job as manager of the bank in Abbeyleix." He sighed. "So she had to give up her career and move with me to the country. Not that she *had* to marry me, but we had other plans. I was to try to get a bank job in London, and she'd take the job with that American company. But then you happened and, well, we didn't think the London plan would work with a family."

"But she didn't mind, did she?"

He looked out over the garden. "I don't know. She said she didn't. She seemed very happy about her pregnancy and everything, and she was excited about moving to the country and buying the house. When you were born she was over-joyed. Never saw such a dedicated mother. But sometimes I could sense she was disappointed. Frustrated, I suppose. She got a part-time job at the chemists' when you started school, but that was small potatoes compared to what she gave up—for me."

"And me," I said when he paused. I put my elbows on the table and looked at him. "So that's why you have been so ambitious for me. You never told me all this before."

He shrugged. "I always felt guilty that she had to give up a great future. I didn't want to dwell on it. Maybe I didn't want you to know. I was afraid you'd blame me or something."

"I would never blame you." I put my hand on his. "Oh, Daddy, don't be sad. I'm sure Mum was happy. We all make our own choices in life, which to others might not be perfect.

Mum wanted a family more than a career. I feel happier in Ireland running this little newspaper than I would be living in London and running a high-profile publication. The *Country Weekend* magazine is going to do very well, but maybe that's also small potatoes compared to the high profile I might have had in London literary circles. The important thing is not to look back."

He took my hand and kissed it. "You're wiser than your years." He sighed. "I suppose I should stop trying to push you. You're old enough to make your own mistakes."

"It's not a mistake. I know I'm doing the right thing. I must stay to save the paper. You see, part of their plan was to hire an editor-in-chief from the UK when I had left. They—I mean the Montgomery Group—were going to make our publication British instead of Irish."

"But you stopped them and made them rehire you? How did you do that?"

I felt my face flush. "Never mind. I just did by using a devious plan. But now they're selling the newspaper. I've heard this new publishing group are bidding for it."

Dad looked alarmed. "New group? Do you know who they are?"

Suddenly hungry, I picked up a wedge of pizza. "No. They're called The Jersean Group. Never heard of them. Can't find anything on the web about them either. I'm a little worried that they might be a cover for something else. Something political."

Dad laughed. "Don't be silly. I'm sure they're just some nice Irish people wanting to get into country publishing."

"You're such an innocent, Dad."

He winked. "Not as innocent as you think, darlin'."

"What do you mean? What are you up to?"

"Can't talk about it yet. It's too soon. I'll tell you later." He bent down to pick up Cat, who was nudging his leg under the table. "You're not the only devious one in this family."

"Does this have anything to do with Liz?"

He stroked Cat. "In a way."

"I haven't seen her for a week or so. Is she away?"

"Yes. She had some…business to attend to in Dublin."

"I see." I studied him for a while, putting my pizza down. He didn't look like a man in love, more like someone going through a crisis. I stopped chewing. "What's going on with you and Liz, Dad? Is it getting serious?"

He nodded, still holding Cat. "Yes. And no."

"How do you mean?"

He looked at me across Cat's back, stroking her soft fur. "I don't know how to explain it. I…oh dear. Audrey, I'm so afraid."

"Afraid of loving again?" I asked, my voice gentle. "In case something happened to her and then…"

He nodded, his eyes full of fear. "I can't go through all that again—all the grieving and sorrow. I don't know what to do." He let Cat down on the grass. "That makes me a big chicken, I suppose."

"No, it doesn't. It makes you human." I reached across the wobbly table and grabbed his hand. "Look at me," I ordered.

He met my gaze. "I'm looking."

"And listen, too, okay?"

He nodded.

I took a deep breath. "Carpe diem, Dad. There is only the present—this moment in time. Liz said this to me a while ago, and she was right. You have to cherish the moment. If you love her, dare to follow through. Dare to show her that love, and dare to be happy, even if it's only for a moment, a day, a week. We don't know what's going to happen in the future, and worrying won't change that. If the worst should happen, at least you'll have had that happiness, those moments together. I mean," I continued, my eyes brimming with tears, "you wouldn't have wanted not to have those years with Mum, would you? Or me, or all the things you did and said to each other. Those memories are gifts that life gives you. Don't refuse them by being scared. It's been—how long? Twenty-five years? You have to let Mum go."

He stared at me in silence. Then he pulled his hand away. "You're right. Thank you."

"You're welcome, Dad."

He coughed. "That's enough of that, then. Any more beer?"

I got up. "I'll get you some from the fridge."

I went to the kitchen to find the beer, walked back into the garden, and handed him the bottle. "There you go." I sat down again. "I hope you realise that I won't be moving out of this flat. I mean, if you're still selling your house, you'll have nowhere to go. Maybe you should wait a while?"

"Too late. It's already on the market." He smiled and winked. "But don't worry, I might have something else lined up that will suit my plans better."

"Those plans you refuse to tell me about?"

"Exactly," Dad replied, looking smug.

I was relieved to see him looking more positive. I only wished there was as easy a solution to my own heartache.

* * *

I heard nothing from Finola for over a week. We were busy covering all the late summer events of the town and even venturing into neighbouring counties to vary our reporting in order to appeal to a wider readership. We were also drawing up plans for the biggest country event in Ireland, in September: the ploughing championships, held in Borris-in-Ossory this year. That was where we'd connect with all the different counties and truly represent rural Ireland. It was also the event where politicians, including the top people of the government, went to lobby for votes and increased support for their party.

Finola asked if she could come with me when she popped into the office one evening. "I'm good at spotting conspiracies and hugger-mugger. This could be when we'll discover the truth behind this takeover of the paper."

"How?" I asked, mystified. "I mean, the ploughing championships? It's like a huge agricultural market, isn't it? Ploughing, sheep shearing, that kind of thing. I know politicians go there to press the flesh of their farming voters, but—"

"That's not all there is to it. Everybody goes there," Finola stated. "And if you have a pint or two with some of the grass roots people, you can find out a lot."

"I don't drink pints."

"Hell, no, of course not." She laughed raucously. "But I do. In any case, I need a break from running after the kids all day. Three-year-old girls sure can cover a lot of ground. I found them chasing hens this morning. Jules wasn't too happy. Her best hens will probably lay scrambled eggs tonight."

"Okay," I said as I shut down my computer. "The championships start on the fifteenth of September. In two weeks. Why don't we go with Fidelma and Dan? I'll just go for an hour or two, but you could stay on and mingle. Then I can come back to the office and finish the layout and get the photos and features as they come in by e-mail. That would save a lot of time. Ploughing isn't really my scene anyway."

Finola's eyes lit up. "Brilliant. I'll park the twins with this terrific local girl I've found who's the best babysitter. She's the eldest of seven and knows how to deal with little terrors like ours. She's been a good solution for us. Doesn't live in but available whenever we need her. A real godsend. I think she's saved our marriage, to be honest. Now we're both free to do our thing, and then we meet in the evenings to play happy families. No more pressure."

"Sounds perfect. What are you going to do with all the free time?"

Finola shrugged. "Don't know yet. But I'll find something. Maybe at the ploughing championships. Who knows?"

"It's not exactly the London Book Fair," I remarked. "Just a hick event for country bumpkins."

"Don't underestimate it," Finola said darkly. "You could meet your destiny at the ploughing championships."

* * *

I tried to stop worrying about Dad and continued asking around for any information about The Jersean Group. Jerry just shook his head and shrugged and my contact woman at Keatings swore she had no idea and asked me to keep her posted. I finally ended up at Jules' one afternoon talking to Rory about the whole issue. We were in the conservatory having tea with Dessie, who was lying on the sofa, her stomach sticking up.

"I'm getting a bit worried about this," I said to Rory, who was rubbing Dessie's feet.

"Why are you worried?" he asked.

"Because they might be connected to these politicians who are trying to spread anti-Europe propaganda. If they buy the paper, they might start ordering me around and telling me to publish opinion pieces or something. Or even fire us all just like Kit said he would."

"Do you really think it'll come to that?" Dessie sighed and put her other foot in Rory's lap. "Do this one too, and don't forget my ankles."

"Of course, sweetheart." Rory rubbed the other foot. He turned to me. "I wouldn't worry until they actually do it. It'll take time to raise the cash and to go through all the legal channels. Might take longer than usual if they're new and don't know the ropes."

Dessie lifted her head from the pillows. "Just like us. We don't have a clue about having a baby. But in about a week or so, we'll find out pretty damn quick what it's like, and then we'll have to cope. "

"Running a publishing group is slightly different from having a baby, as far as I know," I said. "You're not having twins, are you?"

Dessie laughed and rubbed her belly. "No. There's only one in there, but a big one by the looks of it. The doctor said it's 'a good weight,' whatever that means. Probably that it'll be bloody murder to get him out. Or her. Not looking forward to that."

"I'm sure you'll be fine," I soothed. "Not that I'm an expert, of course."

"Neither are we," Rory stated. "By the way, have you been over to my house to look at what Finola and Colin are doing?"

"Not yet. But I think I'll ask Finola to bring me over. I don't want to snoop or anything. I was surprised they left LA just like that," I continued. "Finola mentioned something about her visa and Guantanamo Bay a few months ago in an e-mail, but I thought she was joking."

"Not a joke," Dessie replied. "They might have been in trouble with the immigration authorities. Finola hadn't bothered to apply for a resident visa. But Colin also wanted to move back. Most of his movies are shot in Europe, so LA is a bit far."

"And now they're turning my house into a mansion," Rory cut in. "Don't know what was wrong with it, actually."

"Come on, Rory, the house is a bit of a wreck," Dessie argued. "It's going to be amazing. It'll be redone from top to bottom, and they're adding an indoor swimming pool and gym. They'll have ponies for the girls, so they'll build new stables too, and the grounds around the garden will be landscaped. It'll cost millions, of course, but sure they can afford it."

"Sounds terrific," I said. "It's fabulous to have Finola back here. She's working on a book about the US political situation."

"Yes," Rory agreed, "and her agent has put her proposal up for auction with several publishers."

"There's plenty for her to chew on over here too." I got up. "I have to go."

"You have a date?" Dessie asked, her eyes sparkling.

"Me?" I rolled my eyes. "Nah. Dateable men are pretty rare around here."

"What about Jonathan O'Regan?" Dessie winked. "I thought he seemed *very* interested in you at the party here in June. He looked really upset when he spotted you under the trees in a clinch with your boss."

I shuddered. "Please. Don't remind me. Too much wine that night, I'm afraid."

Dessie giggled and put her hand over her mouth. "Oops. Sorry."

"Never mind. That's all in the past," I assured her. "I've moved on."

"But what about Jonathan?" Dessie insisted. "I sense some kind of romance."

I squirmed. "I haven't time for romance. In any case, Jonathan has gone back to the Iron Age in County Meath. Don't expect to see him until November, if even then. See ye later lads," I said and skipped out the door before Dessie could ask more questions.

Dessie's words had brought back the pain and confusion about my relationship with Jonathan, and it all rushed back as I drove home. He hadn't been in touch since I slammed the door in his face, but why would he? If anyone had done that to me, I wouldn't want to talk to them either. I should have apologised, but I couldn't bear looking at his face or even hearing his voice. Lucky Clodagh. She obviously had what it took to make Jonathan fall in love. Whatever that was.

CHAPTER 21

I didn't meet my destiny at the ploughing championships. I bumped into someone I had hoped never to see again: Christopher Montgomery—hardly my destiny.

Finola and I were pushing through the packed exhibition area, joking about the dress code at a ploughing championship. She was dressed in a Barbour, jeans, and green wellies, while I had gone for the country house option of a tweed jacket and silk scarf tucked into a white shirt, teamed with dark green trousers.

"Talk about House & Garden," she teased when she picked me up. "Didn't think you'd stoop so low."

"I have to blend, ya know," I replied. "Now I can sample the best jams and scones and they'll think I'm one of the judges."

"They'll bribe you with cake, and you'll have to eat it."

I picked at her jacket. "Barbour? You'll boil in this. Very Horse & Hound, darling."

"I borrowed it from Jules. But I think I might have to take it off. Worst thing to wear whatever the weather. I think it must have been designed to be worn only when it's ten degrees in a soft drizzle. Any other kind of weather and you're either freezing or roasting."

"They were meant to be worn by gamekeepers in the 1890s," I quipped as I scanned the crowd. "Gee, you were right about everyone being here. I just saw the Minister for the Environment being interviewed for RTE News."

"What did I tell you?" Finola pointed to a broad back. "And look, isn't that the publisher? Yours, I mean. Wearing a shiny *new* Barbour. Doesn't he know they're supposed to be old and worn to a frazzle like mine?"

"He has no class at all," I said, trying to hide behind Finola. But I was too tall, and my head stuck up above hers. As if he had heard Finola's last remark over the din, he smiled and started to approach us.

"He's coming here," I hissed. "What'll I do?"

"Nothing," Finola muttered. "I'll take care of him."

Kit reached us. "Hello there," he said and moved as if to kiss my cheek.

I stepped back. "Hi. What are you doing here? Networking?"

He smiled. "Just getting a whiff of Irish country life." His gaze drifted to Finola. "Hello, Ms McGee. We haven't met, but I recognise you from the pictures in the papers. You're famous in Ireland."

Finola nodded. "I spotted you too. You've quite a reputation yourself."

Kit looked at her with false modesty. "Nothing like you, Finola, if I may call you that."

Finola nodded and made a gesture like the Queen at a garden party. "You may."

I let out a giggle.

Kit's gaze drifted back to me. "You look well, Audrey. I like the demure style. So what are you girls up to, here at the ploughing championships?"

I smiled sweetly. "I just wanted to catch up on the latest in sheep shearing and ploughing. For the magazine."

"And I'm keeping an eye on what's going down in politics," Finola said. "I have an idea for a new book about how political propaganda is creeping into newspaper publishing."

Kit fixed her with a cold stare. "Nothing new in that."

"Perhaps not," Finola drawled, "but I'll have a different slant on it. You might even feature in this one."

Kit took a step back. "I don't like the sound of that. What do I have to do to stay out of it?"

Finola laughed. "Just keep your nose clean, my friend. And don't put anything in writing."

"I'm getting out of Irish country newspapers," Kit announced. "Too difficult to deal with."

Finola smirked. "I bet. If you get involved in politics in Ireland, you'll soon find yourself up to your neck in a lot of shite. And they won't obey orders, especially from across the Irish Sea."

Kit's face turned red. "Yeah, whatever. In any case, I'll be signing a deal with the new owners of *The Knockmealdown News* as soon as they have organised their payment. You'll have new bosses, Audrey. Two of them, to be precise."

I gasped. "You know who they are?"

"Oh, yes. I've known for a while."

"So, who are they?"

He shook his head. "Can't tell you. I promised not to reveal their identities until they announce it themselves. They're putting out a press release next week." He directed a thin smile in my direction. "I think you'll be more than a little surprised. But I must go. Good day, ladies."

"And good riddance to you," Finola muttered when he had strolled off. "What a slimy creep. Except he's kind of sexy." She looked at me. "I felt a flicker of something between you, to be honest."

I felt my cheeks burn. "Yeah, well…Maybe. But that was a long time ago. I can't stand him now."

"You didn't—?"

"God, no. It crossed my mind at a weak moment when I'd had a lot of wine, but I slapped myself down pretty quick."

"Smart move." Finola looked around the exhibition tent.

"Okay, right. Let's separate. You go for the country journalists, and I'll mingle with the guys from the main rags and the TV crowd. It'll be fun to catch up with some of my old colleagues. You could sniff around the farmers' journals people too. You never know. The new crowd might be buying those as well."

"I just have to check on the rest of my crew. They went to watch the ploughing. Dan wanted pictures of the tractors and the fields. This is only the first day, but he said they'll get a good indication of who's going to win it already. Not that I have a clue about any of that," I added. "But he does."

"Thank the Lord for that," Finola said. "Hey, I see Jerry over there."

"He and Miranda have a stand here this year. Their organic business is booming."

"I know. They're hiring more staff too. But Jerry's bored. I'll go and have a chat with him before I get going. Could we agree to meet for lunch at that catering tent we passed on the way here?"

"Okay."

She touched my arm. "See you later. Good luck." She was swallowed up by the crowd in seconds.

I went the opposite way, heading for the stand of the *Irish Farmers Journal*, where I spent a fun half hour chatting with country reporters who gave me the low-down on ploughing, prize heifers, and the size of pigs, but nothing about this elusive publishing group.

I met up with Finola in the catering tent.

"Wow," she said, laughing. "I now know everything about ploughing, milking, and how to shear sheep. And I got free dog-worming tablets and something for ringworm in horses. But not a thing about this bloody publisher. Maybe they don't exist?"

"They must. Kit wouldn't sell out to a phony group. This was a complete waste of time. Talk about barking up the wrong tree."

Finola looked dejected. "Yeah, I know. But, hey, we had fun, right? And we learned a lot. I also caught up with some of my old colleagues. Boy, am I happy I left reporting. Things are tougher than ever. You get sued if you as much as sneeze in the direction of a politician these days."

"The Jersean Group seem to be good at hiding their tracks."

"Looks like it all right. I feel such a failure." Finola sighed and elbowed herself to the counter. "Let's get lunch. You'll find out sooner or later who they are anyway."

"I hope it's sooner rather than later. And I hope that surprise Kit mentioned won't be a horrible shock."

* * *

I arrived back late in the afternoon, having left Dan and Sinead to continue taking pictures and notes while I downloaded what they had already to the computer. Since it was Thursday, we had to work hard to have everything in place for the weekend edition. Fidelma announced we had two more advertisers —big names in home furnishings and gardening, which would give us a welcome financial boost. Feeling a lot more positive, I worked late into the evening with Mary and Fidelma until I was satisfied we'd done enough for a final polish the next day.

My phone rang just as we were finishing up. It was Rory.

"Just to tell you he's here," he panted. "Nearly three weeks late, the little minx."

"Who?" I asked, confused.

"The baby. Our baby," Rory exclaimed. "Dessie gave birth to a boy at Clonmel Hospital two hours ago. Eight pounds five ounces. He has dark hair and brown eyes, and his name's Kieran."

I laughed. "Oh wow! That's great news. Congratulations. When can I see him?"

"Dessie's going home tomorrow. Give us a day or two, and then she'll be happy to receive visitors."

"I'll be over to inspect him then. Congratulations again. You must be so happy."

"Oh yes." Rory sighed. "Dessie was so brave."

"Give her my love."

I hung up and shared the news with the girls, who were excited and pleased for Dessie. We put some money together for a baby present and cards. When everyone had gone home, I stretched and yawned. Time to stop. I saved the files, put a few Post-it notes on Dan's computer screen, and then left, looking forward to a soak in the tub and a glass of wine.

As I left, I glanced at Jonathan's door across the landing, wondering where he was and what he was doing. Then I saw a strip of light under the door. He was home. Maybe this would be a good time to apologise? Better to get it over with and clear the air.

My knees shaking and my heart pounding, I rang the doorbell. There was no sound from inside. But then I heard footsteps. I wiped my clammy hands on my trousers. The door opened, and I came face-to-face with Jonathan.

CHAPTER 22

We stared at each other for a loaded moment. He looked tired and a little dishevelled. I felt a sudden urge to brush his hair from his forehead but stopped myself in time.

"Hi," I said.

He looked at me blankly. "Hi. What… I mean, I thought you'd be back in London."

"I didn't go. I mean, I turned down that job. Long story." I paused. Then I took a deep breath. "I know I behaved badly a few weeks ago when I came back from London. I didn't mean to slam the door in your face, and I want to say sorry and that I hope we can still be friends even if you're in a relationship." I drew breath and waited for a reaction.

He stared at me. "In a—what?"

"Relationship. You know, like on Facebook, I mean, oh, I don't know. You and whatshername—Clodagh."

Jonathan looked bewildered. "In a relationship? Me and Clodagh?"

"Yes. Aren't you?"

"Not the way you think." Jonathan's mouth quivered.

I suddenly couldn't bear looking at him or even being close to him without being able to touch him. "Well, whatever. I have to go now. Hope you can forgive me."

I turned and ran down the stairs, my eyes stinging. Jonathan shouted something I didn't hear. I hurried inside as fast as I could, threw myself on the bed, and buried my face in the pillows, finally letting out my sorrow in noisy sobs. But I stopped when I heard someone coming into the room. I turned around and saw Jonathan.

"What the hell is wrong with you?" he shouted, pulling me up by the shoulders, his eyes blazing with anger.

"How did you get in?"

"You didn't lock the door."

I turned my face to the wall. "Leave me alone."

"Is this about Clodagh?"

"What the feck else do you think it is?" I turned my tear-stained face to him, knowing my eyes were red and swollen, my nose running, and my hair a mess. But what did it matter? "You said so many things," I wept. "That time, before I left for London, that made me believe you had… feelings for me. I thought…I hoped…."

"Thought what?" he asked. "You were going away to take up a new career. So how would that work, if we were—" he coughed "—lovers?"

"I don't know," I sobbed. "I suppose that wouldn't have been so great. But now I'm back, and I'm not going to be working in London after all, and I was so looking forward to telling you, but then I found out about that girl."

He stared at me. "You're not?"

"No," I cried. "I told you. I'm not. But what do you care, anyway? You have Clodagh."

"No I don't."

"What?"

He got up and tore several tissues from the box on the night table and handed them to me. "Here. Blow your nose."

I wiped my eyes and blew my nose noisily. "Thanks. So? You were saying? About Clodagh?"

He smiled and stroked my cheek with his finger. "You were jealous. But there's no need."

"Yeah, okay. I was jealous, so shoot me." I sat up and

leaned against the wall. "You're laughing at me. Please stop looking so bloody smug and tell me what's going on."

"Clodagh isn't my girlfriend, you silly woman. She's an electrician."

"She's an electrician? So that makes it impossible for her to be your girlfriend?"

"No, of course not. Being an electrician wouldn't stop her being my girlfriend. But I'm not interested in her in that way. I'm, uh, interested in *you*." He sighed. "Shit, this is getting complicated."

"You're really good at explaining things, aren't you?" I dabbed at my eyes and let out a sob mixed with laughter. It was all right. He wasn't in love with Clodagh. She wasn't his girlfriend.

"Shut up for a minute." Jonathan sat down on the bed, put his hands on my shoulders, and looked deep into my eyes. "I'm having this house rewired. Clodagh works for the firm that's going to do it. She was here to look around so they could give me a quote. That's all. Mind you, she's very cute. But I'm in love with *you*, not her. Got that?"

I stared at him. "You're in love? With me?"

He sighed. "Yes. God help me, I am."

I smiled. "Me too." I grabbed his shirt and pressed my face against it. "With you."

"That's good." He snaked his warm hand under my hair and put it on the back of my neck. "Did I hear you say you're not going to London to take that job?"

"That's right." I looked at his surprised face and laughed. "Didn't you hear what I said a few minutes ago? I'm not going to London. I'm not going to be editor-in-chief of *The Bluestocking Review*. I'm staying right here to run our little paper and the new magazine."

"How come? What made you change your mind?"

"I didn't like the smell of the Tube."

He nodded. "That's a good reason. But I bet there's something else."

"Lots of things." I snuggled up to him again. "There was a bit of a clash of personalities. I just couldn't accept the terms of my new job, to put it in a nutshell. Dad was devastated when I told him I'm not going to be this hotshot literary editor. But then he calmed down. It'll take him a while to accept it, though."

"I think he has other things on his mind right now."

"Like what?"

"Shh." Jonathan kissed my eyes, then my nose, his mouth finally coming to rest on mine. We kissed for a long time, until that soft mouth went down my neck and even further down. Gentle hands unbuttoned my shirt and Jonathan lay down beside me, easing my shirt and my trousers off while I was busy undressing him. Naked, we slid under the covers, while the cool wind fluttered the curtains and the rain started again, beating against the windows. We made love slowly, our hands and mouths discovering every part of each other's bodies, murmuring, sighing, moving, softly moaning until we lay still catching our breaths.

I smiled, looking into Jonathan's beautiful hazel eyes. "You're very good."

He smiled back. "Thank you. You're not so bad yourself."

I flung back the covers. "How about a shower?"

"Together?"

"Of course." I got out of bed and held out my hand. "Come on."

We stood in the bathtub while the warm water cascaded over us, soaping each other, and then stepped out, drying each other before we got back into bed. Outside, the clouds scattered and the skies cleared. The thin crescent of a new moon rose above the trees, and the evening star glinted in the darkening sky.

I looked out the window. "There's a new moon. My mother always said that if you make a wish to the new moon it'll come true."

He pulled me close. "My wish already did."

"Mine too." I turned to look at him in the gloom. "What'll happen now? With us?"

He kissed my shoulder. "I don't know. Let's just date for a while. Enjoy getting to know each other. Build a relationship. Make love often and have fun."

I relaxed. "Good idea. We have plenty of time." I traced the outline of his face with my finger. Being in bed with Jonathan was so different and new. He was the most considerate man I had ever made love with, my pleasure being as important as his own. Most men rushed things, only thinking of themselves, taking, never giving. With them, it had been just sex. With Jonathan, even this first time, it had been making love in the true sense of the word.

"Will you sleep with me?" I asked.

"I thought I just did."

"I meant sleep-sleep. All night and then have breakfast together."

He laughed softly and put his arms around me. "Sounds good. But I'm hungry. Did you have dinner?"

"No. I kind of forgot." I suddenly felt my stomach rumble. "I haven't got much in the fridge."

"I have lamb cutlets and some veggies sitting on the counter in my kitchen. I could bake some spuds and it'd be enough for two. I was going to have dinner and then call you in London. I needed an explanation. I was wondering what was going on with you."

"But now you know."

"You explained it in the best possible way."

I got out of bed and stretched. "Can you bring the food down here? I have a bottle of red somewhere. I'll light a fire in the living room and we can eat there."

Jonathan jumped out of bed and pulled on his jeans and shirt. "That'll be grand. I won't be a tick."

I put on my dressing gown and busied myself with lighting the fire and opening the bottle of wine. Cat decided to honour us with her presence and settled on a cushion by the fireplace. "I think I've found the one," I told her. "You know, the man I want to be with and who wants to be with me. He seems gentle, but he grabbed my heart so hard it hurt. In a good way, though. You know what I mean?"

Cat closed her eyes and started to purr. She understood and approved, she said in her unspoken way. I watched the flames flickering around the logs while I waited for Jonathan. We had come a long way in a short time. I only wished everything else was as easy to fix.

* * *

The next morning, as we were having breakfast, I had to make a few phone calls to get the staff started on the ploughing feature.

"Mary, will you get Dan going on the layout and get him to put all the photos in a file? I wrote up an article that's to go with them, and you'll find that in Dropbox in a file marked 'ploughing.' The adverts for the gardening firm and that other one with the cattle feed can go on the same page. Just draw up a rough draft, and we'll finish it when I get there. And please tell Fidelma and Sinead to type in their reports immediately. No coffee breaks today, is that clear? Thanks a million, you're a brick." I hung up and smiled at Jonathan across the kitchen table. "Sorry. I just wanted to get things going so I don't have to rush." I lifted the teapot. "More tea?"

Jonathan laughed and pushed his cup toward me. "I've never seen you in action. You're a tough old boot, aren't you?"

I filled our cups. "In business maybe. But in private I'm a sweet little lamb."

"So you are. But the tough businesswoman kind of

turned me on."

I had to laugh. "Really? Pity I can't throw you on the floor and ravish you right now. But I have to go upstairs and get that magazine out."

"I know. But could you hold that attitude until tonight?"

I winked. "I'll do my best." I felt a sudden dart of joy as I thought of our night together. This was only the beginning. It would get better and better, I was sure of that. "You're unique," I said. "Not many men are like you. I'm so glad I found you."

"Me too." Jonathan studied me for a moment with a hesitant look. "What about that guy? The one you were snogging that night? Sorry, but I need to know what went on there."

I felt my face flush. "Nothing went on at all. Never did. Ever. That night I had too much to drink and was feeling— okay, randy. But I fought him off. You must have seen that too."

"Yes, of course. But still…"

"And he was my boss. I'd never sleep with my boss in any case, even if he was Brad Pitt." I reached across the table and took Jonathan's hand. "Listen, Christopher Montgomery is a domineering prick who wants women to swoon at his feet. I admit he's a very sexy man, but not the kind of man I'd like to have anything to do with. Please believe me."

Jonathan kissed my hand. "I do. Sorry about that. But I needed to know."

"Of course you did." I sighed and poured myself another cup of tea. "I didn't tell you the whole story, and I haven't the time right now. But to put it in just a few words, he was trying to manipulate me to get me to dance to his tune. Politically, I mean. Jesus, I was such an eejit to be taken in by him." I looked lovingly at Jonathan. "Thanks for rescuing me."

"You're welcome." He finished his tea and got up, carrying the breakfast dishes to the sink. "I have to go, but I'll wash up if you like."

I waved him away. "Nah, it's just a few cups and plates. I know you have to get going on that new project and then prepare your lecture for that university course. I'll wash up."

He nodded. "Okay. I'll see you tonight. What do you want to do?"

I winked. "I have a few ideas. But before that, maybe we could go and do that tour of Cahir Castle? I'm embarrassed that I've never actually visited it. But now that I have the best tour guide, I thought it would be a great opportunity."

"It's a date. I could even use my influence as a historian and get us in after they close. Then we can watch the sun set over the Galtee Mountains from the tower. How's that?"

"Fantastic. Oh, and by the way," I added as he was on his way out, "have you heard of this publishing outfit called The Jersean Group? It appears they might become my new bosses."

He shrugged. "Not my area of expertise, I'm afraid."

"I suppose." I picked up my phone. "I'll see if I can find them on Google. I tried before but found nothing."

Google and other searches still came up with nothing. How odd. I was beginning to feel strange vibes. Politics creeping into country papers, Majella said. Were politicians hiding behind this new publishing group?

CHAPTER 23

The sunset viewed from the tower of Cahir Castle was spectacular. As we stood in the tower of the thirteenth-century castle, I felt transported in time. The cool wind whipped my hair as I looked out across the purple slopes of the Galtee Mountains. I could nearly smell the campfires of the soldiers besieging this fortress built on an island by a weir in the River Suir. I could hear the water gushing over the stones and running in under the old bridge and imagined people walking across it on their way to market. I felt the whispers of weeping over dead bodies but also the faint laughter of young women waving at their beaus in the courtyard below the tower. I sighed and leaned against Jonathan, watching the sun slowly set in a riot of colours, while the swallows chirped and fluttered all around us. The sky was a deep blue with orange and pink streaks that stretched all the way to the Knockmealdown Mountains on the other side of town. I shivered, not from the cool breeze but from all those memories floating around in the air like wisps of smoke.

Jonathan put his arms around me from behind. "Cold?"

"No. It's all those little whispers in the air. I always feel the vibes of the spirits in these old places. Maybe the suffering left something in the stones?"

"I know what you mean," Jonathan murmured in my ear. "There was a lot of fighting and killing here. Did you see the cannonball embedded in the wall of the garden? That's from the siege in 1599. James Butler, who owned the castle then, led the rebellion here against Queen Elizabeth's forces headed by the Earl of Essex. The siege lasted only three days, and then Essex stormed the castle with all his men. Poor James Butler had to jump into the Suir to save himself. The English demolished part of the walls and killed a whole lot of men."

"And the women?" I asked. "Was there a Mrs Butler?"

"Yes, there was. I think her name was Anne. Must look it up. Maybe there's a story there that could go into the "Romance Through History" series? Anyway, Essex came to a sticky end eventually. He was running around all over Ireland organising these little raids, and when he didn't succeed in crushing the Irish, Elizabeth had him banned from her court when he went back to England, and had his head chopped off for treason."

"Served him right."

Then Jonathan started to sing softly in my ear, a song that always gives me goosebumps.

And come tell me Sean O'Farrell, tell me why you hurry so
Hush a bhuachaill, hush and listen and his cheeks were all aglow
I bear orders from the captain, get you ready quick and soon
For the pikes must be together at the rising of the moon

At the rising of the moon, at the rising of the moon
For the pikes must be together at the rising of the moon
And come tell me Sean O'Farrell, where the gathering is to be
At the old spot by the river quite well known to you and me...

He sang the whole song right to the end while he held me in his arms. "Not from that era, but about the Battle of Ballyellis in 1798."

"I know," I whispered. "I love it. So sad. I bet many Irishmen died in that battle." I sighed. "I love you, Jonathan. I truly do."

"Why do you love me, my darling?"

"Because you seem to be able to see into my soul. And because you, like a true friend, know how to walk a mile in my shoes."

He didn't answer at first, and he didn't crack a joke about walking in high heels, which made him even more loveable. Then he said, "That's beautiful. You walked a mile in mine too, when you listened to my story that very first night we had dinner."

I turned around and touched his cheek. "It was meant to be. You and me—just waiting to happen."

"Oh yes. Absolutely." He pulled away and held out his hand. "But it's getting chilly, and it's nearly dark. We'd better get down these stairs while we can still see, or we'll break our necks."

I took his hand. "That would be a pity."

We carefully picked our way down the winding stairs, holding on to the rope attached to the old wall and walked across the lawn to the massive entrance door. Jonathan turned the huge key and handed it to the girl waiting in the reception area. We thanked her and headed down the gangway, walking across the empty street to the little restaurant overlooking the river. We got a table by the window and sat down, looking out over the water glinting in the dusk. As Jonathan ordered wine and nibbles for us both, I studied him surreptitiously. He had changed since we'd first met a few months ago. Gone were the stiff manners and slightly hesitant voice, replaced by a more confident air and relaxed posture.

I smiled as he looked at me. "I was just thinking that you're a different person to that polite but distant academic I met earlier in the summer."

He looked surprised. "Am I? Maybe it's because I was a little intimidated by you that first time."

I laughed. "You? Intimidated by me? You're the TV star. I'm just a small-town girl."

Jonathan shook his head. "You're a lot more than that. When you walked into my apartment, I felt like the sun was shining straight at me. And then you stayed, and we talked and talked."

"And I felt I had found a friend for life." I put my hand on his. "Didn't you?"

His eyes were tender. "I did. Very much so. But I didn't know how to take the way you treated me. Like a brother or someone you liked but couldn't fancy. I thought you were afraid of men or something. And then you were cuddling up to that creep who was your boss. I thought—"

I put my hands on my hot cheeks. "Please, don't remind me. That was an accident. Okay, so I admit I kind of fancied him, but that was only my hormones or something. I actually loathe him, as you know. I'm trying to forget all that."

"I know. Sorry. Shouldn't have brought it up again. But it took a lot of control not to go and punch him in the face that night."

I had to laugh at the image of Jonathan getting into a fist fight with Kit. "I wonder who'd have won? Kit's quite fit. Works out in the gym and all. Probably just to look good."

Jonathan joined in my laughter. "I can throw a good punch when I'm provoked, you know. Did a little boxing at university. But never mind that. No postmortems, okay?"

"Absolutely not. Or I might have to bring up your fling with that hot little TV producer."

It was his turn to look uncomfortable. "God forbid. That was also a kind of accident."

I smirked. "Hmm. Really?"

"Do we have to go there?"

"Let's not." I picked up my glass and took a sip. My eyes drifted to a group of three people at the far wall of the restaurant. I hadn't noticed them before, so they must have arrived before us. Now I saw who they were. Dad, Liz—and someone else, whose back was to me. I couldn't see who he was, as he was partly obscured by a pillar. They were having an animated discussion and looking at pieces of paper spread out on the table.

"Do you want another glass of wine?" Jonathan asked.

"No thanks." I kept staring at the group. "Look," I muttered. "Dad and Liz."

"Are they out on a date too?" Jonathan said, glancing in their direction.

"Doesn't look like it. Who's the guy with them?"

"Can't see. Too dark."

I craned my neck to see better. "They're arguing about something."

Jonathan took my arm. "Let's go. They're obviously not on a date, but maybe they don't want to be noticed. Why else would they meet here and not at the usual pub in Clough-michael?"

"Maybe they're buying a house together?" I mused. "I mean they've been pretty sweet on each other all summer. They might be planning to—"

"Come on," Jonathan urged. "I've paid the bill. Let's continue our date. It was going so well."

I stood and picked up my handbag. "Okay. Sorry, just my journalist nose twitching."

"A very pretty nose," Jonathan said as we walked outside. He pulled me close and kissed me. "And now I'm going to take you to my lair and ravish you, my lady."

"Oh, please do, my lord," I simpered.

"First, more wine on the terrace. Then, bed."

"Perfect," I whispered against his soft mouth.

We walked hand in hand to his car, the cool wind caressing my bare arms. It was a beautiful early autumn night. Perfect for making love. But as we drove off, my mind drifted to Dad and Liz. They had looked serious, almost worried. Something was going on with them. But what?

* * *

"It's your birthday tomorrow," Dad said on the phone the following Monday.

"Oh my God, is it? I had completely forgotten."

"You'll be thirty-three," Dad chortled. "I'm throwing you a party at Killybeg."

"A party?" I glanced at my reflection in the hall mirror. Thirty-three. Were those little lines wrinkles? I moved, and the lines disappeared. Just shadows. "You don't have to do that. I'll just have dinner with you and Liz. And Jonathan."

"Jonathan?"

"Yes. We're…dating."

"That's good news. He's a good lad," Dad said at the other end. "But the party is not only for your birthday, it's for something else too, that we'll reveal then."

"Reveal? Is it you and Liz? Are you—?"

"Seven o'clock," Dad interrupted. "And we're dressing up. Black tie for the men. Bling and glam for the women, Liz says."

"Black tie? Really?"

"See you then," Dad said and hung up.

The plot thickened when I arrived upstairs. All the girls were chatting and laughing, and Dan was on the phone, trying to make himself heard.

I slammed the door shut behind me. "What is going on?" I shouted.

The chatter stopped. "We're going to a party," Mary said. "At Killybeg. Tomorrow."

"We're all invited," Fidelma said.

"And we have to dress up," Sinead announced. "It's black tie, and Dan's trying to hire a tux from the clothes hiring firm in Clonmel."

"Oh?" I looked at them, perplexed. "Did my father invite you?"

"No. It was Jerry Murphy," Mary replied. "There's something big going on, and we're supposed to do a feature, but they didn't say what it was about."

"Jerry?" I asked. "What the hell is going on?"

Dan hung up. "Got a tux, but it's blue. All the black ones were gone. The whole town is going to this event, it seems."

"So what is it in aid of?" I snapped. "Come on, Dan, tell me."

He shrugged, looking sheepish. "Don't know. But we'll find out tomorrow."

"That's not good enough," I muttered and went into my office to call Pandora.

But Pandora didn't know much either. "Your dad has booked the drawing room and ordered a big champagne buffet. He said it was for your birthday and some other big celebration. Are you getting engaged?"

"No, I'm not," I muttered. This whole thing was beginning to get on my nerves.

"Maybe it's your dad, then," Pandora suggested. "Didn't you say he's dating someone? Are *they* getting engaged?"

"I asked, but he said no, that wasn't it. But maybe he lied?"

"You don't have a problem with that?" Pandora enquired. "I mean, she'll be your stepmom, won't she? If they get married, I mean."

"I know. And no, I wouldn't object. I love Liz, and I'd be happy for Dad."

"That's what I thought." Pandora paused. "What could it be then? I mean, he's pulling out all the stops and has invited nearly a hundred guests. The best champagne and our most expensive buffet. This isn't going to be cheap. Not that we mind," she added with a laugh. "We love throwing this kind of party. And I've just booked in a crew from RTE, who're going to cover the event."

"What?" I nearly shouted. "RTE? As in television?"

"Oops. I shouldn't have told you. It's supposed to be a secret."

"Oh God." I sighed. "This is getting weirder and weirder."

"Yes, but exciting too," Pandora remarked. "Hey, why don't you come beforehand and have an hour or two in the spa? I'm going to have a facial and mani-pedi. I'd love you to do it with me. My treat for your birthday."

"That's very sweet of you," I replied. "But tomorrow's a very busy day. The online paper has to be done, and then we have a whole heap of stuff to get through for the magazine on Saturday."

"Yeah, but you have to look stunning at the party," Pandora argued. "How about a mini-facial and make-up half an hour beforehand? You can get dressed in the spa changing rooms. We have a new beautician I hired from New York. She's terrific. She'll make you into a star."

"That sounds great. Okay, I'll be there around six thirty or so. Thank you, Pandora."

"You're welcome," Pandora chirped. "Can't wait. Tomorrow will be really exciting, I promise you."

She hung up before I had a chance to ask what she meant. She obviously knew more than she let on. I realised that I had been completely fooled and sidetracked by a very clever woman. I turned my attention back to work, telling myself I had to stop asking questions and be patient. The secret would be revealed soon enough. The only annoying thing was that I seemed to be the only one in the dark.

CHAPTER 24

I was late for my appointment at the spa. But Cindy, a sweet Asian girl with a New York accent, told me she'd be quick. "Just a little cleansing and buffing, and you'll be ready for the make-up," she said. "Just lie down, close your eyes, and relax. I'll do the rest."

"Wonderful," I said with a sigh. I lay down on the padded bench, closed my eyes, and gave myself up to her skilled hands. I had hung my dress in one of the cubicles in the changing rooms and agreed to meet Jonathan in the bar before we went to the party together. I needed his support for this event.

"You're tense," Cindy said as she laid a soft blanket over me. "And I can see you're stressed. Your skin's a little dry."

"Am I getting wrinkles?" I asked. "I mean, I'm turning thirty-three today, so maybe—"

Cindy laughed softly while she applied something cool to my face. "Thirty-three? But that's young. No, no wrinkles, but just a little dryness here and there. Have you been stressed recently?"

"Yes," I mumbled as my body began to relax. "Very stressed in many ways."

"You should try yoga. Very de-stressing and great for toning everything."

"I should start something." I touched my stomach under

the blanket. It was a little wobbly. I hadn't had much time to go to the gym lately. Yoga might be something worth trying. "I've had a little trouble in my love life, but that's sorted now," I continued. "I just started seeing someone really special. He's not at all my type. But what is a type anyway? I thought mine was a macho kind of guy, but then I learned the hard way that they're not worth it." I stopped, realising I was babbling. "Sorry. Maybe I shouldn't talk so much?"

Cindy continued to massage my face with something that smelled divine. "Talk as much as you want. A lot of my clients do. You have no idea the kind of personal details they tell me. It's as if my touching them makes them feel safe and loved or something. But I don't mind. I love people, and I love to see women relax and feel pampered."

"You're very good at it."

"Thank you. But you were saying?"

I sighed and breathed in the lovely scent. "Oh, nothing really. All is well for the moment. What's the gorgeous smell?"

"A cleansing lotion made with a mixture of fruits and essential oils." Cindy wiped my face with a tissue and applied a cool liquid with a cotton wool ball. "This is a moisturising mask that'll dry in a few minutes. And then I'll remove it and apply a toner and you're done and ready for make-up."

"Sounds good."

"I had this client today," Cindy chatted on. "An older woman. Sixty-ish. Nice skin for her age. She told me all about herself and how she's finally come to terms with how her ex-husband treated her. She's met someone new, she said. Someone who's not only her boyfriend, but also her business partner. They're starting a new venture together. He's put all his savings into it, she said. So they'll be—"

I sat up. "What? Business partner? Was her name Liz?"

Cindy looked at me, surprised. "Yes. That was her name. Great tipper too. Do you know her?"

"Yeah. I know her." What was this all about? Joint business venture? Was Liz conning Dad? "Did she say anything else?" I asked. "I mean, did she explain what kind of business it is or anything like that?"

"No. She didn't go into the details. But you'll probably meet this Liz at the party. You can ask her then."

"Yes, but—"

"Please lie down so I can finish the treatment," Cindy ordered.

"Okay." I lay down again and squeezed my eyes shut, my whole body stiff as a poker.

"Could you try to relax? Or at least not screw up your eyes like that?"

I did my best, while all kinds of thoughts whirled around in my head. Was Liz trying to fool Dad into giving her all his money? Was she some kind of gold-digger? Or a confidence trickster? Or maybe even a black widow, who killed her victims after— I slapped myself down. No, stop it. Liz was divorced, not a widow. Or...? What did I know about her former life? Not much. But Jonathan did.

* * *

"What do you know about Liz?" I asked Jonathan in the bar half an hour later over a champagne cocktail when I was finally all made up and dressed in my slinky black silk dress, my hair swept up.

"You look beautiful," he said, his eyes misty.

"Thank you. So do you," I said, only just noticing how knock-'em-dead gorgeous he looked in a tux. "You should always be in black tie. Always and forever. Cary Grant lives on in you."

He blushed. "What? Are you serious?"

"Perfectly." I knocked back my cocktail. "You should be

dressed like that all the time. But maybe only in private."

He winked. "That could be arranged. But what was that you asked? About Liz?"

I pulled myself up. "Yes. How well do you know her?"

He looked thoughtful. "Quite well. She moved into her flat about two years ago. She told me she needed a place of her own after her divorce. She had retired from the firm they ran together, and since then she's been working freelance as an accountant. Seems to be good at it. They had no children, but she has a sister and nieces and nephews in Dublin she's fond of."

I nodded and wriggled on the bar stool. "Most of that I know too. Anything else?"

"She loves gardening and Irish music, mostly the old, classical stuff. Speaks Irish fluently and—" He stopped. "That's it really. Except that I like her a lot, and she's great company. Good sense of humour and very helpful and easy-going. Why do you ask?"

I fiddled with my glass. "I'm worried. I think she has made Dad invest in some kind of business venture that has eaten up all of his savings, which he planned to live on when he retires."

He stared at me. "What? You think Liz is some kind of gold-digger? I find that hard to believe."

"Me too. But… Okay, so I'm overreacting here. It's just all this secrecy that's getting to me. He has obviously gotten into some business deal. But why hasn't he discussed it with me?"

"Probably because you'd talk him out of it. You'd be all for the safe option of keeping his money stashed away and only using it a little at a time. Like some kind of addition to his pension."

"Yes, that's what I think would be the safest thing. He's worked hard all his life, and now he can relax and take it easy. Maybe even get into that little fixing shop he mentioned.

You know, doing repair jobs and painting and decorating. He loves that kind of work, and he's good at it. Wouldn't that be perfect for him at his age?"

Jonathan shook his head. "He's not an old man, darling, he's only sixty-five. Not ready for the slippers and chair by the fire yet. I'd say he wants to try something new and exciting, maybe even a little risky. And remember, Liz is a qualified accountant with a lot of experience. I'd say she'd be a huge help to him." He touched my cheek. "Try not to worry, okay?"

"Okay," I said without conviction. "I'll try."

We were interrupted by Mary, Fidelma, and Sinead, all dressed to kill in party dresses and high heels. Dan arrived behind them, looking surprisingly trim in his hired tux. Jonathan bought them all drinks, and then we chatted for a while before it was time to join the party down the corridor, which seemed to have started already.

Jonathan took my hand. "We'll soon find out what's going on," he muttered in my ear. "I'm sure it won't be as bad as you think. Your dad's no fool."

I smiled, trying to look positive. "I hope you're right."

We walked down the hallway into the brightly lit drawing room, which had been turned into a party room used for weddings and other social gatherings. The room's lovely Georgian proportions had been enhanced by new paint, curtains, and lighting. The room was packed with people dressed up for serious partying. At the back of the room, Dad and Jerry were testing the sound system, beside which was a huge table where the serving staff were finishing laying the buffet. A cameraman from RTE hoisted a camera onto his shoulder, ready for action.

Pandora, in a red dress that made most of her generous curves, came toward us with two champagne flutes. "Hi. You both look amazing." She leaned forward and kissed me on the cheek. "Happy birthday. Champagne for you both."

"Thank you." I took one of the flutes.

"It's for the toast." Pandora handed Jonathan the other glass. "Jerry will make an announcement as soon as Finola's here."

"And Colin?" I asked.

Pandora shook her head. "Not coming," she said in my ear. "He hates crowds, and he was worried he'd be mobbed by the women at the party. And of course, that's a distinct possibility. Besides, he wants to spend as much time with the girls as he can before he leaves for the movie that's being shot in Norway later this month."

There was a commotion at the door as Finola, in a black pantsuit, pushed through. She made a beeline for me, and as she came closer I could see the excitement in her eyes.

"Hi, Audrey. I just wanted to say that I'm sorry and that I didn't have a chance to tell you before tonight."

"Tell me what?" I asked, confused.

"About—"

But her words were drowned out by Jerry's voice from the loudspeakers. "Ladies and gentlemen and Audrey," he started to general laughter.

"Is she a lady or a gentleman?" someone shouted.

"A lady," Jerry said, "but she's also the birthday girl."

"Happy birthday, Audrey!" shouted a group near the buffet table. They started to sing the birthday song, soon joined by the whole crowd in a nearly deafening chant.

"Thank you very much!" I shouted, forming a megaphone with my hands.

Dad lifted his glass. "A toast to the birthday girl. Cheers, Audrey!"

Everyone gulped down their champagne. This was followed by more singing and applause.

Dad waded through the crowd and planted a big kiss on my cheek. "Many happy returns, girl. I have a present for you, but I'll give it to you later. I have to do something first. I think you'll be pleased." He waded back through the throng to Jerry's side.

Jerry called for order, tapping the microphone. "Now that we've cheered for Audrey, her dad, Mr Sean Killian, wants to make an announcement. Over to you, partner."

"Partner?" I mumbled to Jonathan. "What does he mean?"

"No idea," Jonathan muttered back. "Just listen."

Dad had managed to make his way back to his position beside Jerry, who had been joined by Finola. I spotted Liz standing behind them with a big smile on her face, her eyes on Dad.

"Hello, everyone, and thank you for coming," Dad said. "I'm sure many of you have been wondering what this celebration is all about."

"You bet we have," I muttered.

"Well," Dad said, "it's about the newspaper. *The Knock-mealdown News. Your* newspaper, I should say. As you may or may not have heard, it's been sold by the Montgomery Group to a new publishing firm—The Jersean Group. And who are they, you're probably asking yourself. Well, we can now reveal all. The Jersean Group are—" he paused as we all stared at him with bated breath "—Jerry and me, Sean. Thus, the name. Jer-Sean."

I gasped, feeling I was going to faint.

"Holy shit!" someone shouted.

I squeezed Jonathan's hand so hard he winced. "Oh. My. God. Of course!" I exclaimed. "Why didn't I think of that? How stupid I've been. *That's* what he's been up to."

Jonathan threw back his head and laughed. "That's hilarious. Jerry and Sean. What a crafty pair of old geezers."

Delight mixed with relief, I beamed back at Jonathan. "Jerry is a bit too young to be an old geezer, but not Dad. I'm so happy for him."

Jonathan smiled. "Me too. Let him know how happy you are."

"Well done, Dad!" I shouted and clapped my hands. I was soon joined by most of the guests, who applauded, shouted, and whistled.

"But there's more," Dad continued into the mike. "Please calm down for a second so I can tell you the rest."

The noise died down.

"The road to our purchase has been long and hard," Dad said. "We didn't have sufficient means between the two of us, so we nearly gave up. The bank would only lend us a small amount, and my lump sum plus Jerry's savings didn't quite meet the purchase price." Dad grabbed Liz's hand and pulled her forward. "Our accountant, Liz Mulcahy, advised us to ditch the idea, and we nearly did until a new partner stepped in and added to the pot. This new partner is none other than—Finola McGee. Step forward, Finola."

Finola waved and grabbed the microphone from Dad. "Here I am," she shouted. "This is the most incredible thing I've ever done. But I did it. Never thought I'd end up as part of the establishment. But, Jesus, life's so weird. I had this big advance I didn't know what to do with. Should probably have spent it on plastic surgery to fix my nose and suck the fat out of my thighs. But this seemed a whole lot less painful and a lot more fun. I've missed being in publishing, and I've missed this little town. But now I'm here to stay, and I'll be back in business again. In a different way, of course. But still. I have a foot in there."

The crowd erupted into renewed cheering and shouts of "Good on ye, Finola!"

I stared at Jonathan. "Finola?" I stammered. "But...I mean she and I were trying to figure out... We were a team, I thought. Sleuthing together on the trail of these unknown publishers. And then she was in it all this time."

"Seems a little sneaky, I have to say," Jonathan remarked.

"Sneaky? She lied to me, the conniving bitch. And now she's my boss. Makes me think I was better off before. At least *he* was easier to figure out."

Someone tugged at my arm. "Audrey," Finola said, "I can explain."

I glared at her. "Yeah, right." I knew the camera was aimed at us, but I didn't care. I would have walked away, but Finola held my arm in an iron grip.

"No, you don't. You're going to listen to me."

"Why should I?"

"Because I say so."

"Oh, I forgot," I scathed. "You're my boss now. I'm supposed to curtsey and say, 'Yes, sir.'"

Jonathan grabbed us by the arms and pulled us through the crowd to the door. "Maybe you should continue this, uh, discussion in private? It wouldn't do to have the fight broadcast to the nation."

We made it into the corridor before Finola put her hand on my arm and started to explain. "I know you think I lied to you. But it's not true. I didn't find out about Jerry and your dad until that day at the ploughing championships. When you left, I went to have a chat with Jerry. Just idle gossip, you know? Catching up. A long-time-no-see kind of thing. That's when he told me about what he and Sean were trying to do and how they were short of funds."

I pulled away. "Yeah? And you just forgot to share this with me? It involved my father, but I suppose that didn't occur to you."

Finola nodded. "Yeah, sure it did. But I didn't want to say anything before I had decided. I went home and had a long chat with Colin. The advance for my new book had just come through, and I had a huge cheque for my articles in various US papers in the post. I needed to invest all of that in something that might give me some dividends. Jersean seemed like a good option. Colin added a bit as well. And then, your father—"

"Dad? What about him?"

"He asked me not to tell you. He didn't want you to know until it was a done deal. He was afraid to look foolish if it fell through."

"Foolish? But he's my dad. I love him no matter what."

Finola nodded. "Of course you do. But he wanted your respect and admiration. He wanted you to be proud of him, not sorry for him. He doesn't want to look old and weak. I think men at that age are as worried about growing old as women. Maybe even more so."

My legs suddenly wobbly, I leaned against the wall. "Oh. I didn't think of it like that. God, that makes me feel bad."

Finola's eyes softened. "Don't feel guilty. Not your fault he's so insecure. I think he needed to impress Liz too. During our meetings, he's been trying not to lean on her. She's a strong woman. Smart as a whip. But that's hard for men to take."

"I know. I'd be happy if he ended up with her."

"Me too," Finola declared. She smiled and patted my arm. "Come on, let's go and enjoy the party. And that rather dishy man is hovering at the door, staring at us. Maybe he thought we'd get into a fight?"

I laughed. "If we did, you'd win."

"Nah, you're taller than me. I wouldn't be able to reach."

"You're right, I could just bop you on the head."

"You could. But now it's all sorted, so we can forget about fighting. I'm really looking forward to working with you. You've done such a great job with that magazine." Finola waved at Jonathan. "Come on. She's all yours. I'm going to get some of that delicious nosh before it's all gone. See ye later, lads."

"She's such a powerhouse," Jonathan said as he joined me.

I sighed and blew on a lock of hair. "I know. I'm exhausted after that chat. I don't really want to go in there again. But I should. Just to congratulate Dad."

"How about finding a quiet spot, like the library? Then I can get some food and wine and bring it to you. We can eat in peace, and then maybe your Dad could join us?"

I sighed happily. "That would be perfect. Thank you." I kissed him on the cheek. "See you in the library."

"Won't be long," Jonathan promised.

The library, dimly lit by lamps with green shades, was blissfully quiet. I walked along the bookcases and ran my fingers over the spines of the books, the worn leather as soft as silk. The slightly musty smell evoked pleasant memories of my grandfather's house, where I'd been read tales of magic and adventure from early childhood.

Jonathan returned, carrying two glasses of wine, followed by a waiter with a tray, which he put on a table by one of the velvet sofas.

We sat down and, suddenly hungry, I picked up a fork and started to eat. There was lobster salad, a chicken drumstick, some avocado, and a baked potato with sour cream and chives.

"I had to put it all on one plate," Jonathan said, biting into his chicken leg. "A bit of a strange combo, I suppose."

"It's yummy," I mumbled, my mouth full. "I was starving."

"So I see." He kissed my nose. "You're looking better. You were so pale there in the drawing room. I was getting worried."

I touched his cheek. "So sweet of you to worry. I was scared in there. Didn't know what was going on. Nobody would tell me. Okay, so they wanted it to be a surprise, and Dad was feeling insecure, but it didn't seem fair somehow."

"It wasn't." There was sudden fire in Jonathan's eyes. "They shouldn't have put you through all that. I didn't know what was going on, but if I had, I would have done something about it."

I sighed and picked up my glass. "Well, never mind. It all turned out well in the end, didn't it?"

"It did. But now I want some time for you and me." He pulled a folded piece of paper from the pocket of his tux and handed it to me. "This is your present. Happy birthday, sweetheart."

I unfolded the paper, read what was on it, and gasped. "A cruise for two in the Baltic to St Petersburg? Oh my God, how fantastic!"

Jonathan grinned. "We'll visit the home of Leo Tolstoy too."

I looked at the date of the booking. "We're going at the end of the month? For two weeks? But what'll I do about the paper, the magazine and everything?"

He grinned wickedly. "Let Finola take care of that. Didn't she say she wanted to get back to publishing? And I have a distinct memory of you telling me she handed it all over to you when she married Colin and went to LA. Now it's payback time."

"You're right. I had to jump in at the deep end then." I threw my arms around him. "I have dreamed of doing this trip for years. Thank you, my sweet, adorable best friend."

He kissed me. "And I want to thank you for—" He paused. "For… for, well you know. Everything."

"No need to say thank you. I love you, that's all." I took his hand and pulled him up. "Let's go."

Jonathan resisted. "But what about your dad and everyone? They want to celebrate your birthday. They have presents for you, and there'll be a cake and more singing."

I sighed. "Oh shit, I don't want any of that. Please, Jonathan, take me home. I want to get into bed with you and talk about our trip. And then go to sleep with your arms around me. Screw the others. And, forgive me, but screw Dad too. He's had me long enough. I want to run away from home."

He jumped to his feet. "You're right. We need time for us. Come on, let's sneak out before they spot us. We'll take my car and leave yours here."

We tiptoed across the carpet and peered out the door. The corridor was deserted, and the noise from the party a little less loud than before. "They must be still eating," Jonathan said. "Perfect time to escape. Come on!"

We raced down the corridor, across the lobby, and out into the cool, starlit night. When we reached the car park, we jumped into Jonathan's car and drove off.

When we were just outside town, he pulled into a leeway and turned to me. "I just need to—" He pulled me into his arms and kissed me hard on the mouth. I kissed him back, putting my arms around his neck, and we stayed there, snogging like teenagers until Jonathan pulled back and started the engine. "Now I'm ready for bed. How about you?"

I laughed and squeezed his thigh. "After that kissing marathon? Drive on!"

And he did, possibly breaking the speed limit. Ten minutes later we were naked in bed doing what we'd been wanting to do all evening. And what we would be doing over and over again until death did us part.

THE END

About the author

Susanne O'Leary is the bestselling author of more than twenty novels, mainly in the romantic fiction genre. She has also written three crime novels and two in the historical fiction genre. She has been the wife of a diplomat (still is), a fitness teacher and a translator. She now writes full-time from either of two locations; a rambling house in County Tipperary, Ireland or a little cottage overlooking the Atlantic in Dingle, County Kerry. When she is not scaling the mountains of said counties, keeping fit in the local gym, or doing yoga, she keeps writing, producing a book every six months.

Find out more about Susanne and her books on her website: http://www.susanne-oleary.co.uk

Printed in Great Britain
by Amazon